THE TIMINGILA

Shon Mehta

This novel is entirely a work of fiction. The names, characters, businesses, faiths, places, events, locales, and incidents portrayed in it are either the products of the author's imagination or used in a fictitious manner. Any resemblance to actual persons, living or dead, or actual events is purely coincidental.

Paperback Edition ISBN 978-1-703-02585-9
Electronic Edition ISBN 978-0-692-10803-1
© Sheetal Mehata

Author's website: www.shonmehta.com

To my husband, my anchor – for creating a novel out of my first draft.

To my mother – the strongest person I know.

To my father – for convincing the five year old me that I am the best writer in the world.

CONTENTS

CONTENTS

CONTENTS

01

THE PLACE TO BE

They say that if you are born in Sonira, you won't be jealous of heaven – and if you are born in Igati, you won't be afraid of hell. But for the people of Trishala, their city was their glorious heaven, and it was their living hell.

Trishala was neither Sonira, the most beautiful city in the ancient land of Jivavarta, nor Igati, the frozen hell without reprieve. The people of Trishala loved and hated their city – for them, it had its own charm.

Trishala was a trading port surrounded by three powerful kingdoms: Rongcha in the north, Adrika in the east, and Yashantika in the west. It was so strategically located that whichever kingdom controlled it could control Jivavarta. So, the three kingdoms decided to keep it free, but raided it whenever they thought it was getting too prosperous.

Things changed under current king. When King Vighasa Laznaka came to power, he made a treaty with these kingdoms, stopping the raids in exchange for a yearly tribute. With his diplomacy, he kept these kingdoms at bay, and Trishala flourished.

To celebrate the treaty, the people of Trishala started observing the festival of Varti. Every year, they painted their houses and shops with bright colors, and decorated the streets with lanterns to welcome Thelesa, the Tapasi goddess of trade, wealth, and prosperity.

Tomorrow was Varti, and Trishala was the place to be.

02

TASVAK OF TRISHALA

"Let me go, brothers," Tasvak urged.

Some faces can be confusing – looking at them, one can't really decide whether they are beautiful or ugly. Tasvak's face was not one of them. It took just one look to be certain that it is the ugliest face one has ever seen.

Tasvak was a large young man, around nineteen, with dark hair and pale skin. The deep scars on his face and his piercing green eyes made his appearance intimidating.

His appearance did intimidate his stepbrother, Prince Nahusha, a sickly fellow and the crown prince of Trishala. Nahusha felt that Tasvak's sheer presence undermined his authority, and that made him rather insecure.

Nahusha didn't spare a chance to pick a fight with Tasvak, and beat him with the help of his younger brother Kindisha. The scars on Tasvak's young face were tokens of injuries from such fights.

When he was a kid, Tasvak had tried to reason, but could not understand why his stepbrothers kept bullying him. But he had realized one thing very early – that nobody was going to protect him, not even his father.

The scared little boy had ran to his father, the king, for protection as his stepbrothers came after him. But King Vighasa had brushed him away. Tasvak was born of King Vighasa's momentary affection for a girl of lower birth, a mlechcha. When the king learned about Tasvak being born, he had the girl executed. The king would have killed Tasvak too, but Guru Sarvadni, the Tapasi monk, had convinced him otherwise.

"You can't kill him, he is your son. According to the Tapasi faith, a son carries the blood of the father. He has your blood. If you kill him, it will be a great sin."

The king let Tasvak live, but that didn't stop him from despising his mlechcha son. "Show this mlechcha his place!" he had told his highborn sons. "But take care that he doesn't die. He is my blood, and your stepbrother, after all."

The bullying had continued over the years, and Tasvak had no way out but to fight back. He fought back, because it hurt less than not fighting back.

Today, Nahusha had attacked him under the pretense of wrestling. Tasvak overpowered Nahusha with ease. Seeing this, Kindisha jumped in, and pulled Tasvak over. The two brothers could barely control a raging Tasvak. Although restrained, it looked like Tasvak was the only one who had control of the situation.

"You almost broke Prince Nahusha's hand," said Princess Keya, the king's daughter from his other wife. With her surreal beauty, Keya could charm anyone, except her brothers.

Keya herself was bullied by her stepbrothers, but she never let go of an opportunity to bully Tasvak.

"Tasvak, you son of a mlechcha, you fiend!" shouted Nahusha, kicking Tasvak. He was trying to hide his embarrassment. Kindisha smirked.

Tasvak didn't say anything. He just wanted this to be over.

"Let him go," ordered Nahusha. "He has learned his lesson."

Nahusha was afraid that Tasvak will overpower him again. Better take the high road, he thought.

Kindisha released Tasvak, and warned him, "I am waiting for the day when father won't be there to stop us. Then, you are a dead man."

Tasvak nodded, and walked away.

03

THE CITY OF TRADERS

Despite his family, Tasvak loved Trishala.

Trishala had two parts. The upper part of the town, set on top of a hill, was extremely beautiful. Home to the nobility, with their grand palaces, it was filled with fragrance of flowers from the numerous gardens. The roads were wide and clean, and mostly empty. Once in a while, one could see horseriders, noblemen in their carriages, or their ladies sitting in intricately decorated and luxurious shibikas, carried by servants, with beautiful maids swaying close behind. This part of the town was exclusive to the noblemen, except on Varti, when the commoners were permitted inside to join the festivities and sing praises of the king.

The lower town of Trishala, the part down the hill, was a different story altogether. It was as if someone had meticulously planned the perfect, well-organized town – and then had gone ahead and built the exact opposite.

There was no consistency in anything. Streets of every size and shape went in every direction. One could smell, all at the same time, the fragrances of essences and exotic herbs displayed in the traders' shops, the "Trishala fish" and other delicacies being cooked in the eateries, and the fresh catch being sold at the waterfront. There were shops of all sizes, which sold anything and everything. The reputed traders sold exotic leather, pottery, souvenirs from faraway lands, and Soma, the delicious wine of rich. Right beside, the lesser reputed ones sold stolen goods, suspect antiques, and Sura, the putrid wine of poor. The roads were crowded, and people moved around in carts, chariots, horses, and even elephants, which they could hire for a few extra karshikas.

Tasvak usually spent much of his time moving around the lower town as a commoner. The peace following the treaty had brought to Trishala a steady flow of people, mostly traders, from all over Jivavarta. These people brought along their culture, their traditions, and their religions. Tasvak liked mingling with these people, learning about their lands, and dreamed of visiting those places someday.

But today, he was upset at his brothers, and longed for the calmness of the Nilabha lake.

Amongst all the things in Trishala, he enjoyed his visits to the Nilabha lake the most. The lake was located near the highest point of Trishala, up above the upper town.

From there, Tasvak could see the entire Trishala, the river Girika, the tribal settlement of Idany on the riverside, and the grand Vakshi forest beyond.

Nobody else visited the lake. The people believed that it was haunted. According to the legend, centuries ago, the erstwhile king of Trishala had started building the upper town. As Nilabha lake's steps were being built, the lake's water started receding rapidly. Scared by what appeared to be wrath of Sarvabhu, the supreme Tapasi deity, the king hurriedly sacrificed a mother and her newborn baby by drowning them in the lake. The water stopped receding, and the upper town was built as planned. But over the years, some people reported seeing the woman's ghost, and hearing cries of help deep into the nights.

Nobody knew the truth, but the people of Trishala were terrified of venturing anywhere near the lake. But for Tasvak, the beauty and calmness of the lake far outweighed his fear for the ghost.

After climbing up to the lake, he stood on the steps, closed his eyes, and was about to dive into the water, when he was startled by a shout.

"Stop! Don't jump."

04

THE GIRL AT THE LAKE

"Don't jump, this lake is haunted!"

Tasvak looked in the direction of the voice.

He noticed a girl, about sixteen or seventeen years old, running towards him. She was thin and fragile, her long unruly hair tied into a knot, which was getting untangled as she ran. As she came nearer, Tasvak was struck by her dark skin color, the darkest he had ever seen in Trishala. Her large black eyes made her pretty face even more beautiful.

Tasvak turned back, and prepared to dive. He had no intention of listening to this stranger.

"Believe me, the lake is haunted. You will die as soon as you touch the water," the girl urged, breathlessly, as she approached Tasvak. She had heard so many stories about this lake from her father.

Tasvak wanted to shrug her off, but the genuine concern in her voice amused him.

"Don't worry, I won't die," said Tasvak. He then took a deep breath, and dived headlong into the water.

The girl rushed forward. A swirl had formed on the surface of the lake, right where Tasvak had dived in. She gasped, and waited with bated breath.

When Tasvak emerged after a short lap underwater, the girl was still standing on the steps. She reminded Tasvak of the mahogany statues in the palace.

Seeing Tasvak alive, the girl gave a cry of relief.

"You are not dead!" said the girl. She started giggling, and could not stop.

"I am not," said Tasvak, as he climbed the steps. "I told you not to worry."

His voice was serious, but he could not hold his smile. Not many people in Trishala talked to him so freely.

The girl gave out another giggle. She was feeling nervous, and could not control herself.

"This lake is not on the regular path," said Tasvak. "If you believe that this place is haunted, then what are you doing here?"

"I missed my path," the girl explained. "My father has recently started working in the palace, and I help him. Usually, we walk together from the lower town. Today, he had to leave early, so I walked alone and must have taken the wrong path. I haven't been here ever, but have heard stories from my father."

Tasvak nodded, and sat on the steps. The girl hesitated a bit, and sat down beside him. Tasvak realized that he was still smiling.

"I am Avani. My father is the garlander at the palace. We provide fresh and beautiful garlands. Take this one, it will suit your color." Avani pulled out a garland from her small basket. Tasvak hadn't noticed that she was carrying a basket.

Tasvak looked at the garland. It was made of blue, red, and yellow flowers.

"Take it, I am not going to charge you," insisted Avani. She, too, was smiling now.

Tasvak took the garland. It smelled divine.

"So, who are you?" she asked, abruptly. She had been waiting for Tasvak to introduce himself, but he hadn't.

Tasvak looked at her. He wasn't smiling anymore. Avani wished that she hadn't asked.

"I am Tasvak."

"That's an uncommon name. It's like Ugly Tasvak, but you don't look ugly." Avani glanced at the face to be sure, and bit her tongue.

She realized that she had seen this face earlier at the royal gatherings. She had just called a prince of Trishala ugly, on his face.

But Tasvak knew what she meant. He knew that he had been called Ugly Tasvak behind his back, and sometimes on his face, as an insult. But it had neither bothered him in the past, nor did it today.

"Yes, that's me," said Tasvak.

"Sorry for my intrusion, prince. I should go, my father

must be waiting for me." Saying this, Avani hurried away.

Tasvak looked blankly in her direction for a moment. He then kept the garland aside, closed his eyes, and started meditating.

05

Nothing is Permanent

"Are you ready, prince?" asked Guru Sarvadni.

It was Varti today, and like every year, there was a grand celebration at the palace.

"Yes, Guru," said Tasvak, and touched Sarvadni's feet, seeking his blessings. Guru Sarvadni was a frail man with a kind face. His maroon Tapasi robes enhanced his divine aura.

"May you always be true to yourself," said Guru Sarvadni.

Tasvak felt at peace in Sarvadni's presence. Their relation was far more than that of a teacher and student, it was more like a father and son.

"Let us go," said Guru Sarvadni. "The celebrations are about to start."

As they walked to the palace, Tasvak looked around.

The upper town was a changed place, as commoners were allowed in for the festivities, and the usually empty streets were crowded with people. People were dressed well – sharing the festivities with their king made them feel important. Guards were everywhere, keeping a sharp eye on the commoners.

They reached the palace, and took their seats near the dais, beside the ministers and other nobles. Although Tasvak was a prince, his mlechcha blood forbade him to share the dais with the king.

The dais had a huge statue of Thelesa, the Tapasi deity for the festival, covered with a large yellow garland. The garland reminded Tasvak of someone. He smiled.

Below the statue, on a lavishly decorated throne, sat King Vighasa Laznaka. His first wife, Queen Rihushi, and her two sons, Prince Nahusha and Prince Kindisha, were seated on his left, while his second wife, Queen Sameya, and her daughter, Princess Keya, were seated on his right. Princess Keya noticed Tasvak, and looked away smugly.

Standing beside the throne, keeping the king company, was Minister Kathik. He was grinning, and waving at people in the crowd. Kathik was the chief minister of Trishala, and the master of the ceremonies today. Occasionally, he pointed purposefully at someone, whispered in the king's ear, and rubbed his palms importantly. The king did not seem to care, he sat there motionless.

The people around Tasvak talked about the festival, how it was less brutal than Igati's Prahuti, with its tradition of human sacrifice, but not as beautiful as Sonira's

Lolupa-Krish, which marked the yearly harvest, and not as pious as Vanpore's Dhi, with its plethora of Tapasi rituals. Tasvak had heard about these places since his childhood, and longed to visit them.

"Guru, will you ask the king to let me travel with you?" asked Tasvak.

"I don't think you should travel with me," said Sarvadni. "Your place is here. You are not a monk, you are a prince."

"Prince? I am a mlechcha, a fiend." Tasvak gave a little chuckle as he recalled Nahusha's words from the day before. His guru was the only person in whose company he smiled.

"Don't call yourself names," Guru Sarvadni chastised him.

"Forgive me," said Tasvak. "But will you ask?"

"Yes, I will try," said Sarvadni. "But the king seems to have drunk too much, I doubt whether he is paying attention to anything Minister Kathik is telling him." He nodded in the direction of the king.

In negotiating the treaty, King Vighasa had achieved an impossible feat. He was young then, and with the adulation that followed, he slipped into arrogance. As Trishala prospered, so did his ego, and after a point, he stopped paying heed to any advice. The people didn't mind – for them, he was the savior who had stopped their suffering, and brought peace to the land. Today, as Trishala celebrated his achievements, King Vighasa had decided to face glory in a drunken stupor.

The celebrations began with the priests singing hymns in praise of Goddess Thelesa. A group of singers then sang praises of the king, and implored Thelesa to bless him and Trishala with continued prosperity. Prominent traders from the lower town presented gold and precious stones as offerings to the deity. The chiefs of the various tribal settlements around Trishala wished the king a long life, and offered their tributes, including exotic animal hide, ivory, and other produce. Minister Kathik accepted these offerings on behalf of the king.

This was followed by a troupe of artistes enacting stories on the king's early struggles, and glorious achievements. People watched in awe, and cheered when done, shouting praises for their king.

"King Vighasa has taken ill!" someone shouted.

Tasvak glanced towards the king. He saw the king's body slumped to one side.

Nahusha and Kindisha rushed to the throne, and tried to revive the king. The queens broke into tears as they realized what was happening, and what it meant for them. Princess Keya seemed flustered for a short while, then regained her senses, and commanded Kathik to fetch the court physician.

Tasvak's first instinct was to join his family in this moment of grief, but he realized that he might not be welcome. He stayed where he was, with Guru Sarvadni by his side.

The people were dumbstruck initially. Then, somebody started weeping. Meanwhile, Nahusha called the guards, and told them to cordon off the dais.

Chaos reigned for a moment. Then, the court physician arrived and started examining the body. He fiddled for a while, trying all he could. Finally, he pronounced the king dead.

06

THE AFTERMATH

King Vighasa Laznaka was dead.

Most people had left. Those who remained were weeping for their beloved king. The grand festivities of Varti had turned to dust.

The king's body had been placed upright on the throne, and a large yellow garland, just like the one on the deity's statue, had been placed around his neck. The king looked divine.

Tasvak watched from a distance. He was not mourning for his father. But he was sad for Trishala – the city had lost a great king.

Nahusha and Kindisha were standing beside the throne, as if they were guarding the king's body. Queens Rihushi and Sameya were sitting nearby on the floor, dejected and resigned to their fate. Princess Keya was trying to comfort her mother, but seemed dejected herself.

Suddenly, there was commotion outside. A priest had arrived from the grand temple. He hurriedly approached Minister Kathik, and handed him a message.

Minister Kathik had been standing silently in a corner. He read the message, and with utmost deference, approached Nahusha. After a quiet word with Nahusha, Kathik stepped forward and announced that the funeral will be held that evening itself.

Following the announcement, Kindisha instructed the guards to escort the queens to the grand temple, in preparation for the evening. The queens wept inconsolably, but did not resist.

Kathik stepped back into his corner, and started stroking his beard. The happenings that morning had given him much to brood about.

07

THE FUNERAL

The pyre was set on the banks of river Girika. King Vighasa's body, in full royal attire, was placed in the middle.

Prince Nahusha was standing a few steps away from the pyre, holding a torch. The hot, flickering flames of the torch were making him restless. The four generals of the Trishala army, the adhipas, were standing behind him in full armor, with their swords by their side.

Prince Kindisha, Minister Kathik, and all the other nobles were assembled several steps behind the adhipas. Tasvak and Guru Sarvadni were at the back, with Princess Keya, almost in tears, beside them.

Everyone was waiting for the queens to arrive.

Earlier, Queen Rihushi and Queen Sameya had been escorted to the temple, where as a part of the elaborate rituals, they were made to drink so much Soma that they were barely conscious. Dressed up in the choicest regalia, the queens were now on their way to the pyre in their shibikas, accompanied by priests chanting the name of the Tapasi supreme god Sarvabhu, the creator and the destroyer.

As the shibikas approached the pyre, the chants grew louder. The queens, now in a deep trance, were helped out of the shibikas, and placed on either side of the king's lifeless body – Queen Rihushi on the left, and Queen Sameya on the right.

Princess Keya was horrified, and beside herself with grief.

"Stop!" she screamed. "My father is dead, and now you are taking away my mother. Burning her alive, in the name of tradition!"

Her screams did not reach Nahusha, or the priests, amid all the chanting. Not that it would have helped. The old Tapasi traditions still held strong in her family. But Kindisha, standing short distance away, heard her.

"It is an honor for a woman to die in her husband's pyre, sister," Kindisha shouted back. "My mother is in the pyre, too. I am proud of her sacrifice. By Sarvabhu's grace, she will find her place in the heavens."

"Let me burn you alive, then we will see how much honor you feel through the pain." Keya was furious, but helpless. Tasvak could feel his sister's grief, but was aware that Kindisha was merely echoing what the traditions had taught him. Guru Sarvadni quietly gestured to Kindisha, asking him to let it go.

"Careful, sister, and watch your tongue," thundered Kindisha. "Don't forget that father is not there to protect you anymore. One day, your words will cost your life."

The priests, having completed the final rituals, had asked Nahusha to proceed. Nahusha stepped forward and walked to the head of the pyre, while the adhipas took positions at the four corners. Together, the adhipas raised their swords, turned them over, and with a deafening cry of "Long Live King Vighasa", thrust them into the ground. They waited for a moment, pulled out their swords, and raised them again, now with a cry of "Long Live King Nahusha".

King Nahusha said a silent prayer, hailed the great Sarvabhu, and lighted the pyre.

Keya could not take it anymore. She ran out, sobbing. Kindisha's words had made her realize how vulnerable and helpless she had become. Tasvak and Guru Sarvadni followed her.

"Sorry for your loss, princess," said Guru Sarvadni, as they caught up with her. "I could never understand this inhuman ritual. Human life is too precious to waste this way."

Keya did not respond, and went her way.

This was not the first time Tasvak had heard Sarvadni speak against orthodox Tapasi traditions.

"If you really think so, then why don't you change these rituals?" he asked Sarvadni.

"I can't," replied Guru Sarvadni. "I am only a monk.

I don't hold power against such deep-rooted traditions. Only a king can abolish them."

Tasvak nodded.

"Maybe someday Trishala will get a king who knows better, and is not afraid to confront the past," said Sarvadni, looking at Tasvak.

08

THE REBELLION

When King Nahusha summoned Tasvak to the council room, Tasvak expected the worst. Instead, Nahusha asked him to lead an assault against the Idany settlement.

Idany was a tribal settlement along the banks of the Girika river, on the border between Yashantika and Trishala. Idany's location made it strategically important for Trishala's defense against an attack from Yashantika. Just a few days after Nahusha became the king, the Idany tribals had rebelled against Trishala, asking for independence of their settlement.

"I could have sent one of the adhipas," the king told Tasvak. "But these people, who never rebelled in our father's reign, have rebelled as soon as I became the king. So, this is personal. I want somebody from my family to teach them a lesson."

Tasvak nodded in agreement. He was surprised – this was not the Nahusha he had known. The old Nahusha would never have trusted him with such an important task.

"Idany is a small tribe, just a handful of farmers," said Nahusha. "I will give you thirty men for the attack. You will need to leave tomorrow, at sunrise."

This all sounded good to Tasvak.

"Make an example out of Idany, brother, so that others will think twice before they rebel against us," Nahusha added, before leaving the room.

Excited, Tasvak went straight to Guru Sarvadni, and told him how Nahusha had changed. He also talked about the task Nahusha had trusted him with.

"I am happy for you," said Guru Sarvadni, "but I am also concerned."

"Why?" asked Tasvak. "I am taking thirty soldiers with me. How hard can it be to overpower a small farming tribe?"

Guru Sarvadni shook his head.

"You don't know the Idany people," he said. "They might appear to be simpleton farmers, but they are much more than that. It is almost impossible to win them by force."

Tasvak was listening carefully.

"The Idany people have inhabited those lands since ancient times. They are extremely proud and protective of their land and culture," continued Guru Sarvadni. "They are perceived as hostile because they do not trust others easily."

"If they are that invincible and proud, why did they agree to be a part of Trishala?" asked Tasvak.

"Because King Vighasa won their trust," answered Guru Sarvadni.

"So, the only way for us to win them over is by winning back their trust," said Tasvak, thoughtfully. Guru Sarvadni nodded.

Tasvak realized that the task was not as easy as he had thought.

09

The Emissary

Early the next morning, Tasvak and his troop of thirty soldiers rode to Idany.

The terrain was gentle, and very green. There were dense bushes everywhere along the path. The settlement, basically a village, was a cluster of huts along the banks of river Girika. The place was calm, with women washing clothes along the river, children running around, and elders basking in the sun. Tasvak recalled how pristine this place looked from the hill at the Nilabha lake.

As they entered the settlement, the people around stopped their work, and stared at them with curiosity.

"I am Prince Tasvak of Trishala," Tasvak shouted. "I am here in peace."

A frail, elderly man slowly came out of one of the huts in the front. It was the most brightly decorated hut in the cluster. He announced himself as Bhura, the chief of the Idany tribe.

Tasvak alighted from his horse.

"My respects, Chief Bhura," he said. "I am Prince Tasvak, son of late King Vighasa. I am here as an emissary of King Nahusha."

Chief Bhura did not respond. He and other villagers were looking at the soldiers.

Tasvak asked the his soldiers to move away. He did not see any threat from the unarmed villagers.

"Why have you come?" asked Bhura.

"I have come to pay my respects, Chief Bhura," answered Tasvak, "and ask why you have decided to end your alliance of so many years with Trishala."

"We have decided?" scoffed the chief. "Just three days after Vighasa's death, a messenger from the new king came here. He declared that we will need to pay one-third of our farms' produce as a tax to Trishala."

This was news to Tasvak. Nahusha had not mentioned anything about a tax.

"This is our land," Chief Bhura continued. "Vighasa had come asking for our support against Yashantika. We had given the support on the condition that Trishala will respect our rights on this land and its produce. The new king has breached our trust. We do not want to be with Trishala anymore."

The villagers rallied around their chief.

"We will kill anyone who comes to take our crops," shouted somebody. There was anger, and a sense of betrayal in the voices.

Tasvak raised his hands, and asked them to listen.

"Chief Bhura, there seems to be a misunderstanding," said Tasvak, weighing each word as he spoke. "I assure you, in my capacity as an emissary of King Nahusha, that no such tax has been imposed. Trishala respects, and will continue to respect, all promises made by my father."

Bhura reflected for a moment, then smiled, and hugged Tasvak. The tension in the air had dissolved. He then raised his hands, and clapped thrice.

Tasvak heard swift rustling in the bushes behind him, near where his soldiers had been standing just a moment ago. He turned around to see about fifty tribal warriors, in green camouflage, emerge from the bushes. Tasvak gasped, and quietly thanked Guru Sarvadni.

In the celebrations that followed, Tasvak mentioned to Chief Bhura that he was impressed with the way the Idany warriors had blindsided him and his soldiers. Visibly pleased with the praise, the chief offered Tasvak the support of his warriors whenever he needed.

As he headed back, Tasvak had much to think about. He wondered who could be so jealous of King Nahusha as to incite such a terrible misunderstanding.

On his return, Tasvak reported the day's happenings to the king. Nahusha thanked Tasvak, but it seemed that he was surprised to see him alive.

10

THE WORLD AT HIS FEET

To the north of Trishala lay the gigantic mountain range Sahiya, home to the ancient Rongcha kingdom. With the snow-clad mountains touching the skies, and the vast expanse of frozen terrain beneath, Sahiya was both breathtakingly beautiful, and breathtakingly scary.

Igati, the capital of the Rongcha kingdom, was located on the highest mountain in Sahiya. Towering over Igati, reaching out to the heavens above, stood the Rongcha palace. From the palace, a road spiraled down the mountains, all the way to Trishala. Called the "gold route", it was one of the oldest trade routes in Jivavarta.

In the past, the Sahiya mountains had abundant gold reserves, which made the Rongcha kingdom the richest in Jivavarta at that time. In those days, thousands of carts, loaded with gold, traveled from Igati to Trishala along the gold route. But then, the reserves started to dry up, and the economy faltered. King Dhanveer's extravagance and mismanagement further messed up the finances, and now the kingdom was almost bankrupt.

Rongchas considered their kings as descendants of god who, in the beginning of time, had descended from the heavens with the divine right to rule over all Jivavarta. Dhanveer had become the king at the age of sixteen, and had lived a life of abundance and entitlement. The depleting finances of his kingdom annoyed him.

"Is this all the gold we have left?" shouted Dhanveer. His godlike face was red with anger.

His minister was staring at the floor nervously. The king had a tendency to execute those who brought bad news.

"Indeed, my king, this is all we have left," he replied. "The mines have all dried up."

King Dhanveer was sitting in the council room of the Rongcha palace, overlooking the gold route and the mountains below.

"This is not enough!" Dhanveer was furious. "How are we going to organize Prahuti? How are we going to pay the thousand dancers? How are we going to pay for the sacrifice? No one is going to agree for the sacrifice unless we pay the family!"

Prahuti was a grand festival held every year in Igati. It involved a customary human sacrifice in the honor of the king.

He looked out of the window, and caught a glitter

from one of the temples on the mountainside. The kingdom had numerous temples, of a variety of faiths, located all over the mountains. These temples drew a large number of pilgrims every year.

"Look here, see those temples. They have plenty of gold. Ask them for some." Dhanveer had solved a problem, and was very pleased with himself.

"Good idea, my king," said Nachiketa. "But why ask, when we can raid?"

Nachiketa was the commander of the Rongcha army, and the king's son-in-law. He was so cruel that he had no reason to be ugly, and he was so ugly that he had no reason to be cruel. He was feared and hated by all, except Dhanveer. The king was fond of Nachiketa, and sought his advice in most matters.

The minister was feeling miserable at the idea of raiding a temple. Afraid to speak his mind, he looked pleadingly at Princess Guduchi, the king's daughter and Nachiketa's wife.

Princess Guduchi had taken her father's divine looks, but not his arrogance. Unlike her father and her husband, she was compassionate and thoughtful.

"Father, please do not trouble yourself. We will arrange for the gold in time for Prahuti," said Princess Guduchi, dismissing the minister. The idea of raiding a temple was repulsive, but she had learned not to expect anything better from her husband.

Just then, a guard entered the room, and bowed to the king.

"Speak," said Dhanveer.

"My king, a messenger from Trishala has arrived," said the guard. "King Vighasa is dead, and his son Nahusha is the new king of Trishala."

Dhanveer never liked Vighasa, and could not control his contempt.

"That fool Vighasa had the world at his feet," he said. "But with a belly full of wine, he could not see it."

"This is wonderful news," said Nachiketa. He looked excited.

"How is somebody's death good news?" asked Guduchi. She was finding her husband's behavior even more unpleasant than usual.

Nachiketa ignored Guduchi.

"My king, this is our opportunity to renegotiate with Trishala, and ask them to increase the tribute," said Nachiketa. He had been urging Dhanveer to do so for a while, but Dhanveer had refused as he did not want to annoy King Vighasa.

"I agree," said King Dhanveer. He was feeling rather good about the news now.

"If you permit me, my king, I will leave for Trishala with a hundred soldiers," proposed Nachiketa.

"Why will King Nahusha agree to increase the tribute?" asked Guduchi.

"Because Nahusha is a sickly coward," replied Nachiketa, "and Trishala doesn't have much of an army to stand against the might of the Rongchas."

"If we threaten Trishala, Adrika and Yashantika might

come to its aid." Guduchi was not convinced yet.

"Unlikely, as they have their own troubles to worry about," said Nachiketa. "Also, neither of them will mind an increased tribute, so they may even join us."

Nachiketa seemed to have thought this through. He was getting irritated by his wife's unnecessary objections.

"We will deal with them when we need to." Dhanveer brushed away Guduchi's concerns.

Princess Guduchi had nothing more to say. At the least, this will postpone the raiding of the temples, she thought. She was also glad that Nachiketa will be going away for a while.

"We have no time to waste," said the king. "Leave at the earliest."

Next day, Nachiketa marched down the gold route with his troops. He had no patience for threats and negotiations. Instead, he was ready for plunder.

11

THE MESSENGER

Hetuka was very happy. He felt lucky that his masters at Trishala had selected him to carry the message to Sonira. This was his first assignment after joining as a messenger in Trishala's royal services. At fifteen years, he was the youngest and the least experienced of all the messengers, but was selected for this task because of his fast riding skills.

Hetuka had heard so much about the beauty of Adrika, its capital Sonira, and, of course, the festival of Lolupa-Krish, where young people meet to select their future husbands and wives.

His journey so far had been marvelous. He had traveled past snowy mountains, pristine lakes, and fragrant meadows. He had now reached Kavnagari, a beautiful hamlet on the magnificent Devjal lake. This was his last stop before Sonira.

Hetuka was staying at the only inn in Kavnagari. The inn was small and cozy, though a bit crowded with other travelers.

"How far is Sonira from here?" Hetuka hesitantly asked the innkeeper. The innkeeper was a middle-aged, well-dressed, and important-looking man.

"Not far, just half a day's ride," said the innkeeper, cordially. The friendly tone of the reply was a pleasant surprise for Hetuka.

"Are you in Sonira for business, or pleasure?" asked the innkeeper. "If you don't mind me asking, sir."

Nobody had called Hetuka "sir" ever before. He liked the sound of the word. Hetuka cleared his throat, straightened his back, pulled up his chin, and tried to appear as important as he could.

"Not at all," Hetuka began. "I am on an official assignment from Trishala. I am carrying a message, a very urgent message, for the queen …" He stopped himself, wondering if he hadn't revealed too much.

"Ah, don't worry, sir," said the innkeeper, noticing Hetuka's discomfort. "I am not going to tell anyone. Forgotten already."

Hetuka glanced around for a moment, wondering what to say next.

"Please take some rest, sir. You must be exhausted," said the innkeeper, returning to a normal conversation.

"Not really," Hetuka smiled. "This land is so beautiful that even after such a long journey, I am not tired at all."

"Indeed, sir," the innkeeper agreed, and smiled back. "Our land has this magical effect on the visitors."

After a moment, he added "Your food is on us, sir. This is the least we can do for important guests of our kingdom."

Beautiful land, and excellent people – Hetuka was in love with Adrika.

12

THE THREAT

Next day, Hetuka got up before dawn, and started his journey onward. As he reached Sonira, he was mesmerized by its beauty. Set in a lush green valley, surrounded by a river, Sonira defied description.

The palace was a grand structure that melded seamlessly with nature. Tall pine trees on the back were full of birds, who occasionally took a flight around the palace's dome glimmering in the soft sunlight. The gushing waters of the stream flowing beside the palace added to the serenity.

Hetuka identified himself to the palace guards, mentioning that he was carrying an urgent message for Queen Abhadevi. He was told that the queen was on her "vow of silence" for the day. So her son, Prince Revant, would be seeing him instead.

After a short wait, he was led into a room for an audience with Prince Revant. The prince was in his mid-twenties, with brown hair, pale skin, and a charming appearance.

Hetuka bowed to the prince. He was a bit nervous.

"What news do you bring from Trishala?" asked Prince Revant.

Hetuka informed Revant about the demise of King Vighasa, and handed over a message from the new king of Trishala.

"This is sad news," said Revant. "King Vighasa was a great ruler. I feel your sorrow."

Hetuka waited while Prince Revant read the message.

Revant kept the message aside, and paused for a moment. The frown on his face showed that he did not like what he had just read.

"This needs some thought," said Prince Revant, with a forced smile. "We need to wait for Queen Abhadevi to finish her vow. You will have our reply tomorrow."

Hetuka bowed again, and left.

At the tavern that evening, Hetuka learned that Prince Revant was not the crown prince. His elder brother, Prince Vivant, had left the kingdom several years back. Revant had refused to take his place, hoping that the brother will come back someday.

For Hetuka, this was hard to believe. He tried to imagine Nahusha leaving his throne, and then Kindisha not taking his place. He chuckled at the thought.

The situation in Sonira now was that the queen's

brother-in-law, Briham, was trying to capture the throne. That had not happened so far because of Queen Abhadevi's immense popularity.

Hetuka went to the palace the next morning, and had to wait a few hours before he was called in for an audience with the queen.

"We are sorry for Trishala's loss," said Queen Abhadevi. "But that does not justify this request for decreasing the tribute."

Abhadevi was in her late forties. Her elegance and authority gave her a commanding presence.

"The treaty of Trishala was signed a long time back," she continued. "Trishala is much more prosperous now than it was back then. So, Trishala should increase the tribute instead of asking us to decrease it. We have discussed, and put a figure in this message."

A guard handed Hetuka the message, to be delivered to King Nahusha.

"I hear that Rongcha troops are on their way to Trishala," Queen Abhadevi added. "If Trishala doesn't want a similar treatment from Adrika, they need to pay their dues."

Hetuka bowed to the queen, and hurried out.

13

THE MAGICAL STONE

Hetuka realized the urgency of the situation. The talk of the fearsome Rongcha troops marching towards Trishala scared him. He immediately started on his way back to Trishala.

By nightfall, he was at the Kavnagari inn. He was famished after the long day.

"Welcome, sir!" exclaimed the innkeeper. "So nice to have you back. Did you like Sonira?"

"Thanks," said Hetuka. "I enjoyed Sonira. It is the most beautiful place I have ever seen."

"The food is even better, sir," said the innkeeper, as he led Hetuka to dinner. "I would recommend the Sonira delicacy of Sushbhata today. It is a preparation of rice with fresh fruit and nuts. I think you will like it."

Hetuka loved the dish's rich ingredients. While eating,

he mentioned that he was struck by Adrika's prosperity. The kingdom seemed to be truly blessed.

"Oh, yes," said the innkeeper. "The kingdom is indeed blessed."

"There is a legend that tells why. Would you like to listen?" he asked Hetuka. The inn was less crowded than usual, and it looked like the innkeeper had time to spare.

Hetuka was interested. A story would get his mind off the day's happenings.

"Long, long ago, the kings of Rongcha, Adrika, Yashantika, and Trishala ruled in harmony. There was peace and prosperity everywhere. Then, a great famine happened. Thousands of people died of hunger, and man attacked man for food."

The innkeeper paused for effect. Hetuka was listening.

"The four kings sought the help of a wise man, who told them about a magical stone called Chitrantak. Whichever kingdom possessed Chitrantak would never have any natural calamities such as droughts, floods, earthquakes or famines. Also, the kingdom would never be defeated in an attack."

"That would be very useful," commented Hetuka.

"Very useful, indeed, sir," responded the innkeeper, and continued.

"So, all the kingdoms joined forces, and started mining the mountains of Srodhgiri. After years of digging, they found the magical stone – the Chitrantak. It was decided that Chitrantak will be kept with each kingdom one year at a time. First year with Rongcha, then with Yashantika, then Trishala, then Adrika, and then back to Rongcha, and so on till eternity. That way, each kingdom will have its share of prosperity."

"And that solved all the problems," concluded Hetuka.

"Well, so one would think," said the innkeeper. "But you underestimate human greed."

He took a deep sigh, and resumed the story.

"Rongcha, Yashantika, and Trishala kept their part of the deal. But when it was Adrika's turn, the king refused to hand it over. Other kings attacked, but were defeated because the stone made Adrika invincible. The stone is still hidden in Sonira somewhere. So, no wonder, it is the most prosperous place in all Jivavarta."

"But that is so unlike the people of Adrika!" exclaimed Hetuka. "The people here are so hospitable and kind."

"Indeed, sir," said the innkeeper, accepting the compliment. "Glad you think so."

14

THE VISITORS AT NIGHT

Hetuka woke up with a startle. He couldn't see anything. He couldn't move either. He realized that he was blind-folded, and his hands and feet were tied with a rope.

"Where is the message?" asked a voice, and hit Hetuka at the back of his head.

"Don't hit him," said another voice.

"Forgive me, my lord," said the first voice, and repeated, "Where is the message?"

This time, he listened to his master and did not hit Hetuka.

"In the bag below the bed," mumbled Hetuka. He was still drowsy. Surely, the dinner he ate was laced.

He heard somebody going through his bag. There was a brief pause.

"What amount have they proposed for the yearly tribute?"

"Sixty thousand gold karshikas." Hetuka knew this voice. It was the cordial innkeeper.

"Change it to seventy – no, eighty thousand. And, wait, further write that the tribute should be handed over to Prince Briham of Adrika."

"Yes, my lord," said the innkeeper.

"Be careful, make sure that Nahusha is not able to tell the difference."

"What about him?" asked the innkeeper. "He has heard us."

"You seem to be a smart young man, messenger. If you keep your mouth shut, you will get ten gold karshikas. But if you mention anything about this, you will lose your head. As you know, it is very cheap to hire an assassin in Trishala."

Hetuka nodded, and heard steps recede.

Then, someone untied his hands and feet, and removed the blindfold. It was the innkeeper, smiling cordially as always.

"Apologies for the inconvenience, sir. Please take the advice, and do not speak about this to anyone."

As soon as the innkeeper left, Hetuka hurriedly collected his things and bolted out of the door, vowing never to return again.

He did not feel much love for Adrika anymore.

15

THE TRADITION

Leaving Trishala, the river Girika flowed south. As it entered the sea, it created the great marshlands of Khara. These were the lands of the Vidari tribe.

Covered by shallow pools and tall grass, these marshlands bred a variety of exotic wildlife, both on the land and in the water, which were harvested by the Vidari tribals for animal hide, pearls, and other goods.

The only visitors to this land were traders, who bought the harvested goods, or hunters seeking a price catch of a deer, boar, or even a tiger.

Others stayed away, as these lands were not hospitable for humans. Lethal snakebites were common. Predators lurked everywhere. At some places, the land rose mere inches from the water, while crocodiles swam just below the surface. But these were not the only dangers that awaited an unwary traveler.

Vidari tribals had a long-standing tradition of kidnapping bridegrooms for their daughters. It was a common occurrence – travelers disappeared without a trace, and emerged with a wife and child after months in captivity.

Prince Jivak of Yashantika, in his spirit of adventure, had laughed off these dangers as he came deer-hunting all the way to Khara.

The daughter of Chief Snuhi, the chief of the Vidari tribe, saw Prince Jivak from a distance, and took an immediate liking. She had always wanted to marry a prince.

Chief Snuhi could not refuse the tantrums of his only child. He kidnapped Jivak, and performed the wedding. The prince protested initially, but was soon taken in by his bride's charms, and willingly stayed on.

The consequences were severe. Soldiers from Yashantika started raiding in search of their prince. But when they found Prince Jivak, he refused to go back. He sent back a message saying that he was staying willingly, and asked for the raids to cease.

Instead of ceasing, the Yashantika soldiers came back with greater force. They burned the Vidari villages, and mercilessly seized the tribals, taking them as slaves. Then, they captured Prince Jivak, his wife, and his newborn baby, and took them to Yashantika.

"Bring them back!" pleaded Chief Snuhi's wife, Jivanya. "I told you not to kidnap the prince, but you didn't listen. Now do whatever it takes, but bring them back."

"Yes, it was a mistake," said Snuhi. "But after the wedding, I had told Prince Jivak to go back to Yashantika. He refused, saying that he wants to stay here with us. He said that this was his home now."

Snuhi was trying to console his wife, but she was getting desperate.

"Do something," urged Jivanya. "I want my daughter and my grandson back here, alive."

"This is beyond me now," said Snuhi. "I will go to King Vighasa, and beg him to mediate."

One of the guards stepped in.

"Any news?" asked Chief Snuhi.

"A messenger has arrived from Trishala," replied the guard. "He says that King Vighasa is dead, and his son Nahusha is the new king of Trishala."

Jivanya started crying.

Chief Snuhi knew that King Nahusha was too weak to be of any help. He looked at his wife in despair, and stepped out to think.

16

THE SAGE OF VANPORE

Jaskar Dharman was cleaning his bedchamber. He was teaching his son Yashthi, standing by his side, that doing one's own work was a service to God Sarvabhu.

Jaskar Dharman never kept personal servants. He earned his livelihood by selling his paintings, and lived a pious, frugal life befitting a monk. He wore simple robes, slept on the floor, never touched money, and never ate meat. He followed the rules of his Tapasi faith strictly, and he expected others to do the same.

A palace guard was waiting at the door.

"What is the news?" asked Jaskar Dharman. His voice was deep and calm, and gently reassuring.

The guard bowed before the mighty king of Yashantika.

"A messenger has just arrived, my king," said the

guard. "He brings news that King Vighasa of Trishala has died, and his son Nahusha has been declared the new king."

King Jaskar Dharman nodded, and kept cleaning.

"That drunk old fool," scoffed Prince Yashthi. "Good riddance."

Yashthi was Jaskar Dharman's elder son. Twenty years old, he was a good-looking young man with a proud face, and was always eager to impress his father.

The guard stood quietly.

"Anything else?" the king asked the guard. He had finished the cleaning, and was now preparing for his prayers.

"Yes, my king," replied the guard. "There is news that the Rongchas are marching towards Trishala."

"How dare they!" exclaimed Yashthi, looking at his father. "Rongchas can't be allowed to annex Trishala."

"Is King Dhanveer riding with them?" asked Jaskar Dharman, as he lighted the incense before the statue of Sarvabhu by his bedside.

"No, my king," replied the guard.

"Then who is commanding the Rongcha troops?" asked Jaskar Dharman, now looking directly at the guard.

"Nachiketa, his son-in-law," replied the guard.

"You may go now. Everything will be fine by Sarvabhu's grace," said Jaskar Dharman, as he closed his eyes and bowed before the statue.

After the guard had left, Jaskar Dharman turned towards Yashthi slowly.

"I have told you earlier, my son, and I tell you again," said Jaskar Dharman. "Never let your thoughts out before others."

His voice didn't have any trace of anger. But Yashthi's days of being fooled by his father's kind appearance were long gone. He had seen his father brutally kill men while looking calm, kind, and pious.

"Forgive me, father," said Yashthi. He was scared.

"Patience, my son," smiled Jaskar Dharman. "If Dhanveer is not riding with his troops, then he has no intention to annex Trishala. Let us wait and watch."

17

BLOODLINE

"I am grateful to you, my king, for bringing Jivak back," said Queen Dishadevi. She could not stop smiling.

She had just been informed that the Yashantika troops had brought back her son, his wife, and his child. She was beside herself with joy, and had rushed to her husband.

Jaskar Dharman wanted to live the celibate life of a monk when he was young. But after he ascended the throne, he had to concede to his divine duty of providing a heir. He had married Dishadevi, twenty years younger, when he was in his forties. Despite their difference in age, Dishadevi had been a devoted, dutiful, and loving wife.

"You can meet Jivak after his cleansing," said Jaskar Dharman. He was pleased to see his wife so happy after a long time.

"What about Jivak's wife and son?" asked Dishadevi.

"That mlechcha is not his wife," said Yashthi. He was repeating what his father had told him earlier.

"Where are they?" Dishadevi asked again, fearing the worst.

"The boy is long dead, and the mlechcha has been sent to Kalsajja," replied Yashthi. He had seen his father pronounce the sentence just a few moments back.

Kalsajja was a deep pit on the outskirts of Vanpore. It was meant for carrying out death sentences. The condemned were tied and thrown down the pit, where they died a dark, slow death in the company of corpses.

Dishadevi's heart sank.

"Don't do this, my king!" she begged.

"Father has already given the sentence, mother," said Yashthi, and walked away.

"How can be you so cruel?" Dishadevi asked her husband, trying to hold back her tears. She knew that nothing could be done now.

"We are a divine bloodline which has been kept pure for ages, by the grace of Sarvabhu," said Jaskar Dharman, trying to comfort his wife. "By bearing a child, mixing our blood with hers, the mlechcha had committed a crime against our traditions. She had insulted Sarvabhu, and deserved the harshest sentence."

"Think of your son," said Dishadevi, tears in her eyes. "Think of how difficult his life will be after this loss."

"Jivak will realize his mistake," assured Jaskar Dharman. "Life is not difficult, it is our desires that make life difficult."

Dishadevi sobbed silently as Jaskar Dharman stepped into his bedchamber, and closed the door. It was time for his evening prayers, and he had much to thank Sarvabhu for.

18

ABSOLUTE POWER

It has been almost six months since the Rongchas had arrived in Trishala.

King Nahusha knew that the Trishala army, after years without a war, was too weak to fight the Rongchas. He had allowed them in without any resistance.

In a short time, Nachiketa had virtually taken over the Trishala court, as King Nahusha was too afraid to counter him. He increased Trishala's tribute to Rongcha, which pleased Dhanveer, and also to Adrika and Yashantika, which helped them look away.

Nachiketa had never held such absolute power – not even at Igati, where he needed to keep King Dhanveer in good humor, and watch out for his wife. Now, in Trishala, he could do anything without having to worry about anyone.

That power was in display when, on a visit to the lower town, he spotted a girl. She was sixteen or seventeen years old, and buying flowers. Her dark skin and exotic looks created an aura around her, something that Nachiketa had never seen.

"What's your name, girl?" asked Nachiketa, when his soldiers brought the girl to him.

"I am Avani," said the girl. She was surprised, and nervous.

"Come to the palace and stay with me," said Nachiketa. "You will have good food, good clothes, and good fun."

Avani knew what he meant.

"You are mistaken, my lord," Avani tried to reason. "I am a respectable citizen. My father works at the palace. The king will not like you troubling his citizens this way."

Nachiketa smiled. He was even more interested in the girl now.

"Your king will not mind," he said.

Avani was stunned.

"Pick her up," Nachiketa ordered his soldiers.

In face of danger, the senses get sharper. Avani knew, now or never. Before the Rongcha soldiers could figure out what was happening, she slipped away.

Avani ran, with the Rongcha soldiers behind her. She turned into a small alley. Unable to get the horses in, the Rongcha soldiers got down and chased her on foot. But they couldn't keep up, and soon lost her trail.

Avani reached her home, and breathlessly narrated the happening to her father. Her father realized that the soldiers would be reaching there soon. He asked her to leave immediately for someplace safer.

"But they will capture you, father!" cried Avani.

"Don't worry about me," assured her father. "It is a parent's privilege to die protecting their child, I will go straight to heaven."

"I can't put you in danger," Avani resisted.

Her father got hold of her hand, and dragged her towards the door.

"There is no time to waste," he said, handing her a pouch of karshikas. "Leave this instant, if you have any love for your father."

Avani had never seen her father so desperate in her life. She was petrified.

"Father, come with me," pleaded Avani. "We can run together."

"I can't," said her father. "The guards will recognize me. They have seen me at the palace. Get out of Trishala, and go to Adrika or Yashantika. Go now! My child, run!"

Avani ran out, crying, and with no idea of what to do next. Her mind was unable to comprehend what was happening. Just moments back, she was buying flowers – now, she was homeless, and running for her freedom.

Where should she go? Her relatives were cowards, they will not shelter her. What will happen to her father? Should she run away from Trishala? But where? There were too many questions in her mind.

She hid in a dark alley, and thought about whom to ask for help. After she had made up her mind, she walked to the Nilabha lake, where she had met him once, and hid inside the temple.

19

THE ASSURANCE

Nahusha had kept Tasvak busy, sending him to convince Idany and other tribes to pay the increased taxes. Tasvak was unhappy with Nahusha's cowardice, but complied. He was hoping that Nachiketa and his troops will go back soon, and things will be normal again.

Upset with the turmoil, Tasvak had started visiting the Nilabha lake daily. This morning, as Tasvak reached the lake, he was surprised to see a girl emerge from the temple and approach him. The face seemed familiar.

"Who are you?" asked Tasvak.

"I am Avani," replied the girl. "We met here once."

Tasvak remembered the mahogany statues at the palace, and the fragrant garland. He smiled. He could now recall their brief encounter earlier.

"What are you doing here?" asked Tasvak. "Did you

miss your way to the palace again?"

Avani told him everything, and pleaded with him to protect her and her father. Tasvak didn't know what to say. Nobody had ever depended on him this way.

"I will see what can I do," he assured Avani.

He took Avani to his home, and told his servants to take care of her. He then enquired about Avani's father, and learned that the Rongchas had captured him. Realizing the urgency of the situation, he went straight to King Nahusha's chamber.

"Speak," said Nahusha.

"There is a girl," said Tasvak. "She is in trouble, and has asked me for help. I have promised that I will protect her, but I need your help, brother."

"What is your interest in her?" asked Nahusha.

"Nothing, brother," replied Tasvak. "I barely know her. But she has asked me to protect her from Nachiketa."

Nahusha sat up at the mention of Nachiketa's name.

"I will talk to Nachiketa," he assured Tasvak. "Bring her here, and ask her not to worry. She has my protection."

Tasvak was surprised. He had not expected Nahusha to agree so readily. He went home and told Avani that she was under the king's protection now, and had nothing to worry about. He also gave her the news about her father, and assured her that he will find him soon.

Visibly relieved, Avani was full of gratitude towards Tasvak.

20

THE BROTHERS

Avani accompanied Tasvak to meet King Nahusha. When they entered the palace, Nahusha, Kindisha and Nachiketa were waiting for them.

"This is Avani, brother," said Tasvak. "I told her that she is in your protection now."

"Do you fancy this girl?" asked Nachiketa.

"No, it is not like that," said Tasvak. "She came to me asking for my help, and I promised her that I will protect her."

"Ah, I see," said Nachiketa, looking at Avani. "But your king has promised this mahogany beauty to me."

"But brother, you promised me that she will be safe," said Tasvak. He was looking at Nahusha in disbelief.

Nahusha kept silent. He looked at Nachiketa and smiled.

Tasvak stood there helpless. He could see Avani breaking down.

"Hand the girl over and leave," ordered King Nahusha, looking at Tasvak.

"I can't do that, I promised her," said Tasvak, trying to assure the scared Avani.

"Step aside, you fiend," said Kindisha. "Your promise has no value."

Kindisha started moving towards Avani. This was his chance to impress Nachiketa.

"To get to her, you will have to fight me," said Tasvak, and pushed Kindisha away.

Nachiketa scowled, and stepped back.

Nahusha gestured to his guards. Three of them got hold of Tasvak. Two others held Avani.

"Help me, Prince Tasvak! Please, King Nahusha!" screamed Avani, as she was dragged away. "Let me go!" she pleaded.

Tasvak tried to go after her, but was overpowered by the guards holding him.

"What should we do with this fiend?" asked Kindisha.

Nahusha thought for a moment, and stared at Tasvak with contempt.

"You should have left when I told you to," said Nahusha.

He noticed that Nachiketa was fuming at Tasvak's behavior. In a gesture to make amends, he ordered "Kill him."

Tasvak was stunned. He couldn't believe how casually

his brother had ordered his death.

"Get him trampled by drunk elephants," Nahusha told the guards. "That way, the elephants will take the sin of killing him, not us."

A few more guards stepped in, bound Tasvak with chains, and dragged him out of the palace.

Tasvak was thinking of Avani, and how he had let her down. He cursed himself for believing Nahusha. He should have known better.

He was helpless now, and was certain that he will be dead soon.

21

THE SAVIOR

Tasvak was being carried to the elephants for his execution. He was bound in chains and had a hood over his head, just like a common criminal. He was quiet, having accepted his fate.

Suddenly, the cart that was carrying him stopped. Tasvak recognized Guru Sarvadni's voice.

"Thanks for listening to your old guru," Guru Sarvadni was telling the guards. "I will take him away from Trishala tonight, so nobody has to know."

The guards pulled Tasvak down from the cart, and removed the hood on his head.

Tasvak was at the grand temple, and Guru Sarvadni was standing before him. Rudhata, the guru's trusted pupil, was standing by Sarvadni's side.

The guards removed Tasvak's chains, bowed to the

guru, and hurried away with the cart.

Tasvak realized what had happened. Gratitude in his eyes, he touched Sarvadni's feet.

"May you always be true to yourself," blessed the guru.

Rudhata handed a monk's robe to Tasvak.

"You need to hide here until nightfall," said Sarvadni. "Wear this robe so that no one will suspect you."

"I will, my guru," Tasvak said. "But I need to finish an important task before I leave Trishala."

Sarvadni pondered for a moment.

"Go," he said. "But be careful, and don't get caught. This time, I may not be able to rescue you."

When Tasvak returned, he had a girl with him. The girl looked scared, and reminded Sarvadni of a hatchling he had once rescued.

"Who is she?" asked Sarvadni, kindly.

"Her name is Avani, and she is coming with me," said Tasvak.

Sarvadni called Rudhata, and asked him to get some Tapasi clothes for Avani.

At nightfall, Tasvak, Avani, Rudhata, and Sarvadni arrived at the Trishala dockyard. There, they hired a small boat for the Vakshi trail.

"The boat looks old. But don't worry, it is very sturdy," the boatman assured them. A devout Tapasi, he was pleased to ferry the monks across.

"It is a good thing that you are leaving Trishala tonight," the boatman said, as they left the docks. "I hear that someone killed the Rongcha commander Nachiketa in his chamber a few hours back. His men are now desperately searching everywhere for the killer."

Sarvadni was surprised. He glanced at Tasvak, looking for a clue. Tasvak did not offer any – he just sat quiet and expressionless, gazing at the water below.

"Good riddance," continued the boatman. "Between you and me, sometimes I thought of killing that monster myself. Hopefully, the Rongchas will go back to their mountains now, and Trishala will be normal again."

"Yes, hopefully," said Sarvadni.

Nobody mentioned Nachiketa for the rest of the journey.

22

THE CITY OF PEACE

"Deep inside the grand Vakshi forest, atop a gigantic rock that reaches the sky, lies the ancient monastery town of Vakshi," Guru Sarvadni had told a young Tasvak. "Vakshi has monasteries of all the faiths in Jivavarta. It is the most peaceful place I have ever visited."

Ever since, Tasvak had always wanted to visit Vakshi. But he had never thought that his wish will be fulfilled in such a strange way.

As they approached Vakshi, Tasvak could feel the calmness in the air. His anger was slowly subsiding. He glanced at Avani. She was still gloomy, remembering her father who was killed by Nachiketa's soldiers as they searched for her. Tasvak tried to remember his own father, and felt nothing.

"At Vakshi, you will stay as a commoner," Guru Sarvadni told Tasvak. "You and Avani will join my group of followers. This is only for a few days, while you plan your next step."

After a quick discussion with Rudhata, he added that Avani will stay with a small group of women just outside the Tapasi monastery, while Tasvak will share a hut with a certain monk.

"Who is this monk?" asked Tasvak. "Can we trust him?"

"Yes, we can trust him," assured Sarvadni. "I have known him for some time."

"Is he your pupil?" asked Tasvak. He was curious.

"No, he is not," replied Sarvadni. "He will be an awful pupil, but he is a brilliant teacher. He is the founder of his own faith, which he calls Ajabuhi."

"Ajabuhi?" said Tasvak.

"Ajabuhi means a way of life," explained the guru. "He is the lone follower of his faith, so no one will visit the hut."

Tasvak nodded. He was looking forward to meet this Ajabuhi monk.

23

THE MONK

The hut was modest, but tidily kept.

As Tasvak entered, he saw a monk meditating in a corner. He looked about thirty, and was breathtakingly handsome. His meditative poise, and the transcendent look on his face added to his godlike aura.

Tasvak stood still, careful not to disturb, and wondered what to do next. The monk slowly opened his eyes, and seeing Tasvak, broke into a friendly and reassuring smile. Tasvak felt at ease.

"I am Tasvak," he said. "Guru Sarvadni told me that I can stay with you for few days."

"Welcome, Tasvak," said the monk, kindly. "Please make yourself at home. I am Trivit."

"Is Guru Sarvadni here in Vakshi?" Trivit asked, as he got up.

"Yes, he is staying at the Tapasi monastery," answered Tasvak.

"Then I must go and pay my respects," said Trivit, with a smile, and walked out of the door.

Tasvak was carrying the rug that Rudhata had given him earlier. He spread it on the floor, and lied down. He could hear birds chirping outside, and water rushing in the stream beside the hut. He felt at peace, and before he knew, fell asleep.

When he woke up, Trivit was back, and was cleaning the hut. Tasvak got up, and without speaking a word, started helping. Trivit smiled, and Tasvak nodded back.

24

THE DEBT

Trivit never asked Tasvak any questions about his past. Whenever Tasvak interacted with him, he was always courteous in his response. Their communication never went beyond the necessary. This went on for several days.

One afternoon, while Tasvak was meditating in the hut, Trivit was sleeping. Suddenly, Trivit started mumbling in his sleep, and tears rolled down his face. Concerned, Tasvak gently tapped him on his shoulder. Trivit woke up with a start.

"Forgive me for waking you up," said Tasvak. "But it seems like you were having a bad dream, and were in pain."

"Thank you," said Trivit, looking a little embarrassed. "I hope it didn't disturb you."

"No, it didn't," replied Tasvak.

"Did you hear what I was saying?" asked Trivit, as he got up and composed himself.

"You were mumbling softly, so I could not understand," replied Tasvak. "But I think I caught some mention of Sonira."

"I might have been dreaming of my home," said Trivit. "I am from Sonira."

Tasvak had always been curious about Sonira. He had heard much about the city from the traders he used to meet in Trishala's lower town.

"I have heard so much about Sonira," Tasvak said. "Everybody describes it as surreal. Is it as beautiful as they say?"

Trivit smiled.

"Sonira is indeed surreal, and is beautiful in any weather," said Trivit. "The city lies on an island, rising like a lotus in the middle of a river. There are promenades on all sides, with elaborate sculptures and pretty houses beside them."

He took a moment to collect his thoughts, then continued.

"The best part of Sonira is the Island Palace. It is the most magnificent palace you can lay your eyes on, with halls decorated with murals from various parts of Jivavarta."

"That sounds beautiful," said Avani, who had just walked in.

Tasvak looked at Avani with surprise. This was the first time she had opened up since their arrival in Vakshi.

"Then you should visit it sometime," said Trivit. "The palace is also the home of the Queen of Adrika, who matches Sonira in her elegance and serenity."

Having learned a bit about Trivit, Tasvak felt obliged to tell more about himself. Trivit's longing for his home had made Tasvak nostalgic as well.

"I am from Trishala," said Tasvak.

"Now I know why you have been avoiding people from Trishala here," Trivit laughed.

"I have visited Trishala in the past, but I found the people there very busy and money-minded, even rude," he added. "You seem to be very different."

"I know what you mean," Tasvak said. "But that is not the full picture."

It had taken him a while to understand the city.

"Trishala's people wear a mask during the day, as they work their trades and earn their living," Tasvak explained. "Someone is a merchant, someone is a cook, someone is an artisan. Everyone is busy, and they won't talk to you unless it's for work. They are, as you said, money-minded and rude tradesmen."

Trivit was listening.

"But visit Trishala early in the morning, and you can see the humans behind the masks," Tasvak continued. "They cordially invite you to share their breakfast, ask about your health, and regale you with interesting stories. But then, as soon as the bell tolls, they again put on their masks."

"You love Trishala very deeply," said Trivit, looking at

Tasvak.

Before Tasvak could speak, Avani interrupted the conversation. She was afraid that Tasvak will reveal his identity, and wanted to change the topic.

"I am told that you are well-traveled," said Avani. "Did you visit any interesting place on your travels in Jivavarta?"

Trivit thought for a moment.

"There are many, but one particular place comes to my mind."

"Which one?" asked Avani. She was genuinely curious.

"Kahalava pass," answered Trivit. "It is a pass on the mountain route between Sonira and Trishala."

"I have heard about Kahalava, but don't know much," said Avani. "Except that it is a very scary place, and people are afraid to speak about it."

"Yes, it is indeed scary," said Trivit. "It is called Kahalava because while there, you can hear screams of people being killed. Few people wish to travel there, and fewer ever return. Most people take the Janapatha route instead, even though Janapatha takes twice the time."

Tasvak nodded. He was aware of the Kahalava pass.

"It is home to the fearsome Lokharo tribe," Trivit continued. "Lokharos are protective of their lands, and attack the travelers who pass by. They kill these travelers and take away their heads."

"It is said that the Lokharos cannot be defeated," said Tasvak.

Trivit nodded.

"Lokharos use poisoned weapons, and shields made from the shells of Girika tortoises," he said. "They are very agile, and take pride in martyrdom – this makes them fight so fiercely that they are capable of defeating an army several times bigger than theirs."

He smiled silently for a moment, then added, "I once made the mistake of passing through Kahalava, and was captured by the Lokharos."

"Why didn't they kill you?" asked Avani, and immediately bit her tongue.

"I promised their leader, the mighty Zirosthi, something in return," said Trivit.

"What did you promise?" Tasvak was curious.

"I cannot disclose at the moment," said Trivit. "But it is a debt that I need to repay."

25

THE ADVICE

"So, what have you decided?" asked Guru Sarvadni.

"I know that I owe you my life," said Tasvak. "I tried to convince myself to stay in Vakshi as your follower. But I can't do that, I miss Trishala too much. I want to go back to Trishala."

"I saved your life because it was the right thing to do," said Sarvadni. "The Rongchas are still looking for you and Avani, so staying in Vakshi for long is dangerous. But going back to Trishala is far more dangerous. Nahusha will not leave you alive this time."

"Why should I hide?" asked Tasvak. "I have done nothing wrong. I protected someone from injustice. This is not fair."

"Life is neither fair nor unfair, it is just a life," said the guru.

"I don't care for survival," said Tasvak. "I will go back to Trishala, even if that means fighting Nahusha."

"Why do you want to become a martyr?" asked a voice.

Tasvak was startled to see Trivit at the door. He was back early from his daily errands.

"Don't worry, Tasvak," assured Guru Sarvadni. "You can trust Trivit."

Trivit nodded reassuringly.

"Why do you want to become a martyr?" repeated Trivit, as he came in.

"Because it is the most honorable thing to do," replied Tasvak.

Trivit smiled.

"Do you know who is the hero of a story?" he asked.

"The one who is brave, and fights with honor," replied Tasvak.

"No," said Trivit. "The hero of a story is the one who survives to tell the story."

"What do you suggest?" Tasvak asked impatiently. "Should I not fight? Should I hide like a coward?"

"Currently, you are weak," said Trivit. "So, you should focus on your survival. Remember – survive, thrive, strive."

"I don't understand," said Tasvak.

"Survive, because nothing matters if you don't," Trivit explained. "Once you learn to survive, thrive. Thrive by gaining power and influence. After you thrive, strive. Strive to be the greatest."

Guru Sarvadni nodded. Tasvak was silent for a moment. He had never looked at things that way earlier.

"Then, what do you advise?" he asked, looking at Trivit.

"To go back to Trishala, you will have to dethrone Nahusha," said Trivit. "You need to be at a place where you can hide while you gather support."

Tasvak was feeling a bit uncomfortable. He had so far only thought of fighting Nahusha. This discussion was getting way beyond that.

"You can go to Vanpore," suggested Sarvadni. "It is easier to hide in Vanpore than in Vakshi. Also, you can ask King Jaskar Dharman for his help."

"Why will Jaskar Dharman help?" asked Tasvak. "Nahusha became the king because he had the rightful claim."

"This is a flaw of monarchy," said Trivit. "It sometimes puts undeserving people in power. But then, often these people don't have what it takes to remain in power."

"Nahusha is certainly undeserving," said Tasvak. "But why will King Jaskar Dharman help? He doesn't have a reason to."

"Let Jaskar Dharman answer that question," said Trivit. "There is no harm in trying."

"We can advise, but your decision needs to be yours alone," added Sarvadni, as he rose to leave. "You are the one who is going to face the consequences of your actions. So, decide what you want to do with your life, and act accordingly."

26

THE DECISION

"I have decided," Tasvak informed Guru Sarvadni. "I will leave for Vanpore."

Tasvak had given enough thought on what he really wanted to achieve. He now had a clear goal before him – to replace Nahusha as the king of Trishala. He had convinced himself that Trishala would be far more prosperous under him than under Nahusha or Kindisha. He knew that the journey will not be easy, but he owed this to Trishala.

"What about her?" asked Sarvadni, looking at Avani.

"She stays here as your follower," said Tasvak. Avani nodded in agreement.

"I will be pleased if she stays," said Sarvadni. "But she is not safe here. There is nobody in Vakshi who can protect her from the Rongchas. I think you should take her with you."

"In what capacity will she accompany me?" asked Tasvak.

"She can be your helper," suggested Rudhata.

"Helper for poor man?" said Tasvak. "No one will believe that."

"She can be your mistress," Rudhata suggested again.

"I can't take her as a mistress," said Tasvak. "I hated my father for having my mother as a mistress. I will never do that to a woman."

He looked at Avani. She was standing silently in the corner.

"Instead, if Avani agrees, I can marry her and take her along as my wife."

There was silence. Avani was taken by surprise. Although she was not a mlechcha, she was not a highborn either, and had not expected Tasvak to marry her. Taking her silence as her hesitation, Tasvak stared at the floor, thinking what to say next.

"Avani, if you don't want to be my wife, I will understand," he said, carefully, trying very hard not to show his emotions. "I know you deserve better. But please don't judge me by my looks."

"I have no problem," said Avani, softly.

Tasvak stared at Avani in disbelief.

"It is decided, then. Tomorrow morning, you both will get married, and then leave for Vanpore," said Guru Sarvadni, and hugged Tasvak.

27

THE WAY TO VANPORE

Sarvadni solemnized the marriage early the next morning, in the presence of Rudhata and Trivit. There was no time for a celebration, Avani and Tasvak started towards Vanpore almost immediately.

Rudhata accompanied them through the forest, up to the river Nirika that separated Vakshi and Yashantika. He then arranged for a boat for them to cross the river, and bid them farewell.

Avani and Tasvak got down from the boat on the other side and walked further to the road. They were now in Yashantika.

The road was the main trade route between Yashantika and Trishala, and there were several carts on the road. The carts going from Vanpore to Trishala were loaded with grains, while those from Trishala to Vanpore were loaded with luxury goods. For a few karshikas, some cart owners let other travelers ride with them.

As Tasvak waited for a ride at the side of the road, he looked every bit a part of the crowd. He had even tied a small cloth on his head, just like the other travelers, to protect against the dust.

Tasvak hailed one of the carts headed to Vanpore, and climbed in. The cart owner kept waiting. Wondering why, Tasvak looked behind and saw Avani frantically waving at him. He sheepishly stretched out and helped her in.

"Newly married, I guess," smiled the cart owner.

As the cart started moving, they sat without saying a word to each other. Avani fell asleep almost immediately. Tasvak was alert initially, but soon figured that the cart owner was a reliable man. He looked outside. The landscape was dotted with red tambul trees. They passed through several small villages, and Tasvak saw an occasional herd of cows grazing in the fields. By nightfall, he was tired. He covered his face with the headcloth, and fell asleep.

They reached Vanpore late in the morning the next day. The city was guarded by a tall wall, with sharp nails all over it. Outside the wall, there was deep trench that carried the city's drainage. A narrow, heavily guarded iron door opened into the city.

They were made to alight the cart, and the guards checked the cart extensively. As they entered the gates, they were given copper tokens.

"What are these for?" asked Avani, examining her token.

"Without giving back your token, you can't leave Vanpore," informed the cart owner, as they entered the city. "Guard it with your life."

Vanpore was better planned than Trishala. The roads were wider, cleaner, and less crowded. The shops and houses were neatly laid out by the side. There was a temple at every corner, and each was full of devotees.

"So many temples!" exclaimed Avani.

"Vanpore is called the city of temples," said the cart owner, proudly. "There is a temple here for every Tapasi deity."

After some time, as they went through the market, Avani noticed something very strange.

"I see so few women on the streets," Avani observed. She had lived all her life in Trishala's lower town, where there were more women than men on the streets at any time of the day.

The cart owner was surprised at the observation. He explained that in Vanpore, a highborn woman leaves her home only in the company of her father or husband.

"The women you see on road are mostly servants, the cetas," he told Avani.

Suddenly, the cart owner stopped the cart, closed his eyes and, with his palms covering his face, started mumbling the name of Sarvabhu.

Tasvak and Avani couldn't figure out the reason behind his strange behavior. Then, they noticed a woman with tonsured head walking by the road.

"She is a lowborn widow," said the cart owner, with contempt. "Unlike the highborn women, they don't immolate themselves in their husband's funeral pyre. A very inauspicious sight."

In Trishala, only the royal family practiced the Tapasi ritual of widow immolation. Tasvak remembered his father's funeral, the queens who burned with him, and Princess Keya's screams.

"Where can we rent a place to stay?" Tasvak asked the cart owner.

"Cheap or luxurious?" the cart owner asked back.

Looking at Tasvak and Avani, he had been unable to judge their financial status. They had a wealthy look, but their clothes were rather ordinary.

"As inexpensive as possible," said Tasvak.

"There are some huts by the stream," said the cart owner. "I will drop you there."

He dropped Tasvak and Avani at a relatively quieter part of the city. A stream flowed nearby, and they could see a line of huts by its side.

The landlord showed them one of the smaller huts. It had two rooms, and a growth of wild plants in the front. Avani liked the place, and Tasvak paid a month's rent in advance – it was a mere twenty copper karshikas.

Tasvak was astounded at how quickly they had already settled in this strange, unfamiliar city of Vanpore.

Without saying much, they both got down to work and cleaned up the place. Then, tired, they spread out rugs on the floor and fell asleep.

After a short while, Avani woke up with a start. She found that Tasvak was already awake, and was fighting off mosquitoes. It was a losing battle, though. The mosquitoes of Vanpore were too smart for the fugitive warrior of Trishala.

"Now I know why the rent here is so cheap," said Avani.

They both laughed. This was the first time they felt at ease with each other after their wedding.

28

THE CITY OF TEMPLES

Vanpore was deeply religious at its core. Even more at this time of the year, as the Dhi festival was approaching.

Every day, before dawn, priests went around the neighborhoods, softly chanting hymns and blessing the people. Then, they opened the temple doors, and started the morning prayers as the devotees joined in slowly.

After the morning prayers, chanting started. The chanting was accompanied by rituals honoring a deity, a different deity on each day of the week. The chanting went on till sunset. Occasionally, there were processions on the street as well.

After dusk, the temples glittered as numerous lamps were lit in time for the evening prayers. The evening prayers were attended by an even larger number of devotees, and lasted till late.

Even though the entire day was a celebration, it was not for everybody. Cetas and Dhatakis were forbidden from entering the temples, and from taking part in the processions.

Cetas were the slaves. The prosperous residents of the city, the grahavars, owned them. Cetas were freely bought and sold by the grahavars, and worked for their masters without any wages – their masters fed them, used them, and even killed them at pleasure.

And then there were the Dhatakis, the filth cleaners. There was a Dhataki settlement just outside the city, one of the many spread throughout Yashantika. It was believed that people who commit unforgivable sins were reborn as Dhatakis, and were condemned to a life of cleaning filth. They were lesser than humans, and were treated as such. They were allowed inside the city only during the night, and had to complete their work before sunrise. Nobody interacted with the Dhatakis. Nobody even acknowledged them, not even the cetas, because it was a sin to do so.

This was the way of life Vanpore had always known. But for Tasvak, an outsider, the contradictions were apparent. He saw the need for change.

But then, he recalled Trivit's advice. Hiding in Vanpore, being a part of this society, was necessary for him to survive. As he survived, he needed to first make an effort to thrive, by gaining power with the help of Jaskar Dharman. Only after he thrives should he strive to change the order of things.

There was no time to waste. He needed to meet King Jaskar Dharman.

29

BHUYARI

Tasvak had been visiting the palace for the past several days, trying to meet King Jaskar Dharman. He could neither disclose his identity, nor the purpose of the meeting to the guards. So, every day, he was among hundreds of commoners in line to meet the king. As a resourceless outsider, with no contacts in the palace, Tasvak never got a chance.

There is a difference between imagining hardship, and actually facing it. Tasvak had known that his task in Vanpore will not be easy. But now, after several days of effort, he was losing hope. The small amount of money he and Avani had was fast running out. The hardship had left him depressed, and he wanted to get away from everything. He thought of exploring Bhuyari.

Bhuyari was the network of tunnels beneath Vanpore.

It was the city's underbelly, full of poverty and vice, and certainly not a place for the innocent. At Vakshi, when telling about Vanpore, Guru Sarvadni had asked him to stay away from Bhuyari. But Tasvak did not care anymore.

Tasvak was shocked at the sudden contrast as he descended into the dark tunnels of Bhuyari. Unlike the pristine roads above, the tunnels were crowded and filthy, and there was stench everywhere. The tunnels were full of beggars, drunks, and criminals – nobody knew of which birth. In Bhuyari, everybody was equal. There were no cetas, and no grahavars.

"You look sad," said a man, accosting him from behind.

He was a hefty man with a kind face. Tasvak ignored him.

"Try sharing your sorrows, my friend," insisted the man. "You will feel better."

"Yes, I am sad today," replied Tasvak. "I am facing some problems."

The man introduced himself as Peje, the owner of a small tavern around the corner.

"Tell me about your problems," said Peje, in a friendly voice. "Maybe I can help."

Tasvak hesitated, but gave in. This was the first time that someone in Vanpore had shown him empathy.

"I am in need of money, is there is any way I can earn it here?" Tasvak asked, softly.

Peje pondered carefully for a moment.

"To make money, you need money," said Peje. "Do you have any, my friend?"

"Not much," Tasvak said. "Just a little, actually."

"Good," said Peje. "Do you know to play Dutya?"

Dutya was a dice game, a favorite with gamblers.

"I know, but I am not an expert," said Tasvak. He had sometimes played it for fun back in Trishala.

"You don't need to be an expert, my friend," said Peje. "All you need is luck. I have seen people walk to a table with one copper karshika, and leave with a thousand gold karshikas."

"Really?" asked Tasvak.

"Why would I lie to you, my friend?" said Peje.

Peje led Tasvak to his tavern. Both sat on a table towards the back, and started playing.

Tasvak won the first round. He was elated. But then he lost, and lost again, and soon lost all he had. Dejected, he rose to leave.

"You need to pay your debt, my friend," said Peje. His voice did not sound too friendly now.

"I have lost everything I had," said Tasvak, looking at Peje. "Down to the last karshika."

"Don't lie," said Peje.

"No, Peje," said Tasvak, "I am telling the truth."

He was taken aback by the sudden change in Peje's tone.

"Search him!" ordered Peje, as his servants took hold of Tasvak.

The servants searched Tasvak, but found nothing.

"You can't get away by paying so less," said Peje. "Pay now, or else I will make you pay."

"Hey, lay off the poor man," said a voice. "You can't blame a man for giving you less, if you ask him more than what he has."

The voice belonged to a tall, dark man, about thirty years old, or maybe a little older.

"I agree, Viraj," said Peje, the friendly tone back in his voice. "But then, he shouldn't have gambled. Nobody forced him to."

"What else you have?" Viraj asked Tasvak. "You must have something valuable. Believe me, you don't want to mess up with Peje. He is a dangerous man."

"I have nothing," said Tasvak. "I have lost whatever I had. But I can work here until I repay your debt."

"If I start hiring every man who owes me, I will have more servants and less customers." said Peje.

He then looked at his servants.

"Go with him, and check his house for valuables," ordered Peje.

"Can you go with them?" Peje asked Viraj. "I will pay you. He is a large man. My servants might not be able handle him if he attacks them."

The servants and Viraj accompanied Tasvak to his hut.

Avani opened the door. She was surprised to see so many strangers with Tasvak.

They all entered the hut. The servants started searching for valuables, but found nothing.

"He was telling the truth," said one of the servants.

"There are hardly any valuables."

"We will take his wife as a ceta," said other servant. "Master won't be pleased if we go back empty handed."

"You can't take her, she has nothing to do with my debt," Tasvak protested.

"Isn't she your wife?" asked the servant.

"Yes, she is," said Tasvak.

"Then she is your property," said the servant. "The law of the land permits us to take her with us. If you want, we can go to the city officer."

Avani started trembling at the thought of becoming a ceta. She looked at Tasvak helplessly.

"Let her go," said Viraj. "Tell Peje that Viraj will pay this man's debt."

The servants found this strange, but left quietly.

"I am grateful," said Tasvak. He was also confused, and embarrassed.

"Don't worry," said Viraj. "Pay me back later."

They were silent for a moment.

"So, who are you?" asked Viraj. "I have never seen you in Bhuyari before."

"I repent of every moment I spent there," said Tasvak. He stole an apologetic glance at Avani, who was standing in the corner.

"I am sure you do," laughed Viraj. "Sinning and repenting are the favorite pastimes of the people in Vanpore. But, tell again, who are you?"

"I am, um, Tasu," said Tasvak. "And she is my wife, Vani."

"Tasu and Vani," Viraj nodded. "You don't seem to be from around here. Where are you from, and what brings you to Vanpore?"

"We are from Vakshi," replied Tasvak, "and we are here to meet the king."

"That's new." Viraj seemed suspicious. "Vakshi is city of monks. There are not many married couples in Vakshi. Why do you want to meet the king?"

"We are from a small village near Trishala," Tasvak clarified. "We are followers of a Tapasi monk in Vakshi, and are here carrying his message for the king."

He was trying his best to appear normal. Lying did not come naturally to him. He added that he had been desperately trying to meet the king, but had been unable to get an audience for the past several days.

"You are not being given an audience with the king?". Viraj looked surprised. "Did you tell the guards that you have come all the way from Vakshi, and have a message from a Tapasi monk?"

"No, I didn't mention that," said Tasvak. "I didn't know that would help."

"The king respects Tapasi monks, and gives them priority," said Viraj. "Come to the palace tomorrow morning, and give my reference. You will be able to meet the king."

He then nodded at Avani and Tasvak, and left.

Tasvak was baffled at what had just happened. But things seemed to be looking up again.

30

THE AUDIENCE

Viraj fulfilled his promise, and secured Tasvak an audience with the king.

Tasvak was led into the council room. The room was sparsely furnished, with statues of various deities adorning the front wall, and looked more like a temple than a council room. A frail, kindly man in simple robes was sitting on a rug in the corner, with a few guards standing beside.

Tasvak recognized King Jaskar Dharman, and bowed to him.

"Speak, messenger," said the king.

"I bring greetings from Guru Sarvadni," said Tasvak. "I also have a confidential message."

"I have a lot of respect for Guru Sarvadni," said Jaskar Dharman. "My son Jivak was his pupil."

He gestured to his guards, who immediately left the room. Tasvak and Jaskar Dharman were alone now.

"What is the message?" asked the king. "Hope all is well."

"I am Tasvak, son of late King Vighasa Laznaka of Trishala," Tasvak introduced himself. "Guru Sarvadni asked me to meet you and request your help."

If Jaskar Dharman was surprised, it did not show on his face.

"What help do you need, Prince Tasvak?" he asked.

Tasvak related the happenings at Trishala.

"King Nahusha is a puppet in the hands of the Rongchas," said Tasvak. "I need your help in liberating Trishala."

The king closed his eyes and pondered for a moment. He then looked at Tasvak and smiled.

"Why should I help you, Prince Tasvak?" asked Jaskar Dharman. "Trishala is still paying its tribute. In fact, the tribute has increased since the Rongchas took over Trishala. So, why should I have a problem with the Rongchas making Nahusha their puppet?"

"Soon, the Rongchas may annex Trishala, and stop the tribute," Tasvak tried to reason.

"When that happens, I will decide," said Jaskar Dharman. Tasvak realized that any further reasoning will not change the king's decision.

"Convey my warm regards to Guru Sarvadni," said the king, and closed his eyes.

The conversation was over.

31

THE PROTECTOR

When Tasvak came out, Viraj could see the disappointment on his face. He sensed that the meeting had not gone well.

But before Viraj could say anything, Tasvak told him that he was going home.

As he walked, Tasvak kept wondering about how they will survive. Their savings had run out, and he had lost all that remained in Bhuyari. In his thoughts, he did not notice that somebody was following him.

Tasvak reached home, and lied down on the bed. He was very tired, and fell asleep almost immediately.

Suddenly, a stranger entered the hut, pounced on the sleeping Tasvak, and gripped his neck.

"Don't move," said the attacker.

Tasvak didn't move.

"What is your name?" asked the attacker.

"Tasu."

"Lie again, and you are dead," said the attacker, and tightened his grip. Tasvak was pinned to the ground, so could not retaliate.

"Are you the prince of Trishala?" asked the attacker.

"Let him go," screamed Avani. She was standing behind the attacker, with a knife at the man's throat.

The attacker had not expected this. He looked at Avani and didn't think much of her.

"You are weak, and you are scared," he said. "You can't kill a fly. Drop the knife."

"I am weak, and I am scared," said Avani. "But I am here, and I have this knife. Let him go – or I will cut your throat."

It was a convincing threat. But the attacker was not convinced.

"Give me that knife, you foolish woman," he screamed, and tried to grab the knife. In doing so, he loosened his grip on Tasvak.

Tasvak took the opportunity, and pushed the attacker's hand away. Having found his feet, it did not take Tasvak too long to overpower the man. With Avani's help, he tied him up.

The attacker was in a shock. But so was Tasvak. He could never have imagined that someone as vulnerable as Avani could hold a weapon. Until that moment, he had looked at himself as Avani's protector. But today, Avani had been his protector.

There was a knock on the door.

"Who is it?" asked Tasvak, getting on his feet, ready to face another attack.

"It's Viraj. Open the door."

Tasvak reluctantly opened the door.

As he entered, Viraj saw the attacker tied up in the corner. Tasvak explained what had happened.

Viraj approached the attacker, and grabbed his throat.

"You tried to kill my friend," he thundered.

The attacker panicked.

"I am sorry," he said. "I was doing as I was told. I have nothing against this man."

Viraj tightened his grip.

"Please spare my life," pleaded the attacker. "I have small children."

"So, I should spare your life because you have children?" asked Viraj. "Maybe you are the worst father they can have. Maybe they are better off without you."

The attacker was visibly frightened. He was gasping for breath.

Viraj slowly loosened his grip.

"Tell your master that this man is under my protection," said Viraj. "If you come near this man again, you will not go back alive. Is that clear?"

The attacker nodded.

Viraj untied the attacker, gave the man one last stare, and let him go.

"Thank you, master Viraj," murmured the attacker, and rushed out of the door.

"You knew that man!" Tasvak was surprised.

"Yes, I did," said Viraj. "I will tell you all about me in a moment, I promise. But first, tell me who are you?"

"I am Tasu," replied Tasvak. "You know me, I am just a commoner."

"I know now that you are not a commoner," said Viraj. "A commoner doesn't try so hard to prove that he is a commoner. Also, nobody sends an assassin after a commoner. So, again, who are you?"

Avani looked at Tasvak. He nodded.

"He is Tasvak, a prince of Trishala," Avani said. "He killed a Rongcha commander to save my life. Now, King Nahusha of Trishala and the Rongchas are after him."

"I was lying low," said Tasvak. "But now, I am going to destroy them."

He had been suppressing his rage so far.

"How?" asked Viraj. "I don't see an army."

"I have support of the people of Trishala," said Tasvak.

"Are the people of Trishala going to fight for you?" scoffed Viraj. "From what I heard, they did not even fight the Rongchas."

Tasvak kept quiet. The rage was wearing out, and the reality of his situation struck him.

"Let me guess," said Viraj. "You came here to ask King Jaskar Dharman's help, and he has declined."

"He will agree once Guru Sarvadni comes to Vanpore," said Tasvak.

"If you say so, Prince Tasvak," said Viraj. "Meanwhile, you have my word, you are safe here now."

"You just told the attacker to stay away," said Avani. "Why would these people listen to you?"

"Because I am myself an assassin," said Viraj.

"Assassin?" said Tasvak.

"I could have never have guessed," said Avani.

"Even my victims can't, until I kill them," smiled Viraj. "Then they know."

"So, are you now going to kill me?" asked Tasvak. "As you can see, there is a reward for my head."

He was serious.

"If I kill you now, they will give me a few karshikas," said Viraj. "But if you become the king, you may make me your chief minister."

"It's a long shot," Tasvak responded.

"I will take it," said Viraj.

There was silence for a moment.

"You promised to tell about yourself," reminded Tasvak. At the moment, Viraj knew all about him, and he did not know anything about Viraj – except that he was an assassin, who might or might not be a friend.

"I lost my home and my family to plague," said Viraj. "I had a sister and a nephew, her son. But most likely, they are dead too. That's all there is."

"So, where is your home now?" asked Avani. "Where do you belong?"

"Don't worry, I am not a spy from Trishala," smiled Viraj. "Where do I belong? That's hard to answer."

He paused for a moment, as he pondered the question.

"What if I don't belong anywhere?" asked Viraj. "What if I don't fit in any place? It's not that I didn't try. But then, I realized that I don't want to belong to any one place. I want to live free."

Tasvak nodded. Viraj's free spirit was apparent ever since he had met him.

"So, to answer your question," concluded Viraj, "I have no family, and I belong nowhere. Today, I live in Vanpore. Tomorrow is another day."

"That is some serious thought," said Avani. She was happy that things had turned out well.

"That reminds me of why I came here," said Viraj.

He looked at Tasvak.

"You looked very serious when you left the palace today," he said. "If you don't mind me asking, how are you surviving without any money?"

Viraj knew that Tasvak had lost his money to Peje, and having searched the house with Peje's men, also knew that he did not have any savings.

"Barely, as you can see," said Tasvak. "If I had money, then I could have done something."

"Do something, then you will have money," quipped Viraj. "I can find work for you, if you want."

"I will be grateful," said Tasvak. He sincerely felt indebted to Viraj.

"Don't be grateful," laughed Viraj. "I will be doing this for myself. I expect you to repay me generously when you become the king of Trishala."

"I only know how to fight," said Tasvak. "Who wants

to hire a fighter?"

"Fighting for money is not permitted in Vanpore," said Viraj, thinking aloud. "Wait, can you hunt?"

"Yes, I can," said Tasvak.

"I know a few wealthy merchants who want to brag about hunting, but cannot hunt," said Viraj. "Maybe you can hunt for them, and let them take the credit."

"Sure," said Tasvak. "As long as I get paid for that."

"That should not be a problem," assured Viraj, as he left. "You have no idea how much people can pay for a few moments of glory."

32

FALLING IN LOVE

Viraj kept his promise again, and found a hunting assignment for Tasvak.

As he received his payment, Tasvak looked at the glittering silver karshikas in his hand. This was the first time that he had earned money. He had earned it with his hard work.

He felt tremendous happiness, and wanted to share it with Avani. He brought her a set of bangles, and went straight home.

Avani opened the door.

"You are late, I was getting worried," she said. "Wait, you are drenched. Change your clothes, or you will fall ill."

Tasvak had not noticed the rain. He was too engrossed thinking of Avani, and how she will react to his first earnings. He also realized that now there is someone who waits for his return. He smiled.

"Change your clothes," Avani reminded him. "I will give you warm milk and turmeric."

Once they settled, Tasvak showed her the karshikas.

"I earned money today. My first earning. We don't have to live in poverty anymore. I can earn a lot of money this way."

Avani was happy, but looked concerned.

"That is great news," said Avani. "But isn't it dangerous to hunt in the jungle?"

"Less dangerous than staying in Trishala these days," said Tasvak.

"That's true," Avani agreed.

Tasvak took out the gift.

"This is for you," he said, giving her the bangles.

Avani put the bangles on, smiled, and broke into a little dance.

It amused Tasvak. He had seen people dancing at the time of festivals. He had seen dancers in the palace, but they danced because they were paid to dance.

"Is today a festival?" asked Tasvak. "Some celebration?"

Avani laughed, and danced some more.

"I am dancing because I am happy," Avani replied, still laughing. "My husband has given me my first gift after marriage. Is this not enough for a celebration?"

For the first time since they met at the Nilabha lake, Tasvak could hear the liveliness in her voice.

Tasvak had this vague idea about the person who

could be his soulmate. He was sure that this person will forever remain in his imagination, because the existence of such a person was not possible. But now, when he was face to face with her, he didn't know how to behave.

He sensed a warm, fuzzy feeling in his heart, a feeling of overwhelming happiness. He smiled, and gazed at her as she chatted happily. He even thought of straightening her unruly hair.

Tasvak was falling in love with his wife.

33

THE DEVOTED HUSBAND

Tasvak was earning well now. To show their gratitude, Avani and Tasvak invited Viraj for a meal at their place.

"Do you cook this way everyday for your husband?" asked Viraj.

"Yes, I do," replied Avani. "But not so many things. I am not a very good cook."

"It's just that I might not be able to finish the food," said Viraj.

"Why?" asked Avani, hesitantly. "Isn't it any good?"

"Not good?" Viraj sighed. "It is the worst cooked food that I have ever eaten."

"But my husband eats this every day," said Avani.

"Clearly, your husband loves you very much," said Viraj, looking at Tasvak.

Viraj could see the troubled look on Tasvak's face, but

he could not force himself to eat another morsel. He did realize, though, that he had insulted his hostess.

He looked at Avani, and was surprised to find her laughing.

"I knew that," said Avani. "Sometimes, I myself couldn't eat my cooking. But my devoted husband kept assuring me that I am a very good cook. I believed him."

"Perhaps I can teach you a few local delicacies," Viraj said. "Never underestimate the power of good food. Eating delicious food can be a life changing experience. Sometimes, just the thought of good food can save your life."

"Now, that is an exaggeration," said Tasvak, struggling with his bread. "Eating food can surely save your life. But just the thought? No, I don't think so."

"Getting tortured by the Rongchas is the worst thing that can happen to any person," said Viraj. "While in their captivity, whenever I thought of killing myself, I thought about the dishes I could eat once I escaped from there."

"You were captured by the Rongchas?" asked Avani. She was not laughing anymore.

"Trust me," said Viraj, "that is not something I would wish even for my enemies."

Avani turned pale at the thought. Viraj noticed, but didn't say anything.

Tasvak turned silent, too. He was thinking about how he will teach the Rongchas a fitting lesson someday.

34

The City of Mist

For Tasvak, his time in Vanpore was turning out to be more exciting than he had expected, especially since Viraj had agreed to show him different parts of the Yashantika kingdom. On each trip, he discovered something new.

Once, Viraj took him to Mihika Nagari, a small island city in the middle of river Mihika, on the border of Yashantika and Khara.

They landed on the shore in the afternoon. There was mist everywhere, and the visibility was low. As they entered the city, Tasvak was surprised to find the place completely deserted.

"Why are we here?" asked Tasvak.

"Nostalgia," replied Viraj. "I spent the best time of my life on this little island."

"But there is nobody around," said Tasvak. "Just this

mist."

"This place comes alive at night," said Viraj. "Wait for sometime, and see the magic."

Viraj was right. At night, the place came alive. There was dance, music, food, sura and, of course, the famed mihika herb. They bought some herb, and smoked.

For a short while, the herb took them back in time. Tasvak talked of happier times in Trishala.

"Why do you want to go back to Trishala and risk your life?" asked Viraj. "Vanpore is now good to you. It has given you a good life."

Tasvak let out a deep sigh. Maybe it was because of mihika, but he felt like talking.

"Trishala is my home," said Tasvak. "There were times when I have almost hated it. But now that I am away from Trishala, I yearn to go back."

Viraj sensed how strongly Tasvak felt about Trishala. He promised Tasvak that he will do whatever possible to help him in his quest.

"Don't be so glum," said Viraj, getting up. "Come, I know of a place that will cheer you up."

Tasvak followed Viraj to a small alley. A bunch of nubile young girls stood by the side. They giggled softly on seeing them.

"Go, pick whoever you like," said Viraj.

"No, thanks," said Tasvak, turning away. "Why don't you go ahead? I will wait outside."

Viraj was surprised. "What's wrong?"

"Nothing." said Tasvak. "It's just that I promised myself that I will never be with any woman except Avani. But don't mind me. You go ahead, have fun."

Viraj shrugged. "No, let's go back then. This is not a place for devoted husbands."

"Tell me one thing," said Viraj, as they walked towards their boat. "You have so much love for your wife. But why you don't express it? You always seem so distant."

Tasvak nodded. "I don't know whether my affections are welcome."

"Why do you think so?" asked Viraj.

"How can she love me?" said Tasvak, looking away. "I am so ugly."

"Maybe she doesn't think that you are ugly," said Viraj.

Tasvak did not say anything. They walked silently for a while.

Suddenly, Tasvak noticed a baby crying. A man was sitting by its side, selling mihika, and didn't seem to care.

Tasvak picked up the baby. It was burning with fever.

"I think your baby is sick," Tasvak told the man. "You need to take it to a physician. We are going to Vanpore, you can come with us."

"It is not my baby, and I am not going to spend money on it," said the man. "I found it lying beside the trench outside Vanpore. I thought people will take pity on seeing me with the baby, and buy more herbs from me. But this baby cries so much that it is turning away my customers."

He looked at Tasvak lovingly holding the baby.

"Give me ten copper karshikas, and you can take the baby with you," said the mihika seller.

"No, not interested," said Viraj, walking away.

Tasvak knew that the baby will die if left there. He took out ten copper karshikas, and handed them to the mihika seller.

"This is insane," said Viraj. "It's a huge responsibility. Look how sickly he is."

"I know, but this is the best option he has," said Tasvak, as he cradled the baby in his arms.

When Tasvak reached home the next morning, he was worried how Avani will react to his impulsive decision. To his surprise, Avani was beside herself with joy on seeing the baby.

"Give him to me," said Avani, affectionately. "I will treat him so well, that he will feel better in no time."

Tasvak smiled. Those were the best ten copper karshikas that he had ever spent.

35

THE VICTIMS

Tasvak had been curious about Dhatakis ever since he arrived in Vanpore. He knew that Viraj sometimes visits the Dhataki settlement, and asked if he could accompany him.

"That's a strange request," said Viraj. "Nobody likes to visit the Dhatakis."

"Then why do you go?" asked Tasvak.

"I go for work, to hire cheap assassins," said Viraj. "No matter how highborn a person is, he can't tell an attacker to not touch him because the attacker is a Dhataki."

"I want to know more about them," said Tasvak. "I have seen how unfair it is to be treated badly because of your birth."

"Do you feel sympathy for them?" asked Viraj.

"Dhatakis have to clean the filth of Vanpore, and in return they get a hellish life," Tasvak said. "There is no way out for them. Why? Because in the past, someone decided that Dhatakis don't deserve to be treated as humans."

"Fine, you can accompany me," Viraj relented. "But keep in mind, whenever the history of Vanpore will be written, the Dhatakis won't play any part, except emptying the filth pots."

"Maybe, but what if someday they decide not to play that part?" asked Tasvak.

"If I were you, I would keep those thoughts to myself," warned Viraj, making his displeasure clear. "They are considered treason in Yashantika, and for good reason."

As they entered the Dhataki settlement, Tasvak was shocked by the inhuman living conditions. There was filth and stench everywhere, and malnourished children roamed around in the garbage.

Viraj was there to meet Khoram, the leader of the settlement.

"You are getting greedy, Khoram," said Viraj. "For three boys, you are asking fifteen silver karshikas."

"I am asking fifteen silver karshika for three Dhataki lives," said Khoram.

"I don't understand," said Tasvak. "These boys will be taking lives, not giving their lives."

"Do you think anybody in Vanpore is going to protect a Dhataki assassin?" asked Khoram, leaning forward. "No, these boys are dead for sure. Their families are going to lose their sons, forever. They need more money."

Khoram sounded like a righteous protector of Dhataki

rights, but an occasional smile and the spark in his eyes belied something else. Viraj knew his kind well.

"Khoram, I don't think you are going to give more than a silver karshika each to those families," said Viraj. "You are going to pocket the remaining. Why do you need so much money?"

Khoram looked at Viraj, gave a broad smile, and dropped the pretense.

"I have five daughters," he said. "I need money for their marriage. Fifteen silver karshikas, or the deal is off."

As they left the settlement, Viraj cursed loudly.

"He tells me that he cares for his daughters," said Viraj. "But, given a chance, he will not think twice before selling them, too. The man is nothing but a filthy leech."

"Then why do you deal with him?" asked Tasvak.

"Because he is the leader of his people," answered Viraj. "It might surprise you, but the Dhatakis have a strong social hierarchy among themselves. Khoram is a highborn among the Dhatakis, and so carries a lot of clout among his people."

"But he is a victim of the society's excesses," said Tasvak. "How can he be a bad person?"

"Why not?" said Viraj. "Being a victim doesn't make one virtuous."

Tasvak nodded. He had learned a useful lesson that day.

36

The Final Tribute

When Guru Sarvadni came to Vanpore, it had been more than a year since he had last met Tasvak.

"May you always be true to yourself," said Guru Sarvadni, as Tasvak and Avani bowed before him.

"You are looking so tired, Guru," said Tasvak.

"I am an old monk, and I am getting older," said Sarvadni.

He smiled at the baby in Avani's lap, and looked at Tasvak.

"I am very pleased to see that you both are happy together. In your message, you forgot to mention that you have became parents."

"This baby is not ours," Tasvak explained hastily. "I found him abandoned in Mihika Nagari a few weeks back."

The guru blessed the baby.

"A very noble deed," said Sarvadni. "But the baby might not be safe with you here."

"I agree," said Tasvak. "What do you suggest?"

"You can send him to Vakshi with my pupil, Rudhata," suggested Sarvadni. "The monastery will take care of the baby for you."

Avani and Tasvak reluctantly agreed.

Guru Sarvadni now came to the purpose of his visit.

In his message, Tasvak had told Sarvadni about Jaskar Dharman's refusal to help. Sarvadni had met the king that morning, and had tried to persuade him. Jaskar Dharman had told Sarvadni that he can give Tasvak protection, even a position in his court. But he refused to support Tasvak against Nahusha.

"A few tribes in Trishala might support you," said Sarvadni. "But without Jaskar Dharman's help, attacking Nahusha would be suicidal."

"Stay here," Sarvadni tried to convince Tasvak. "You have a good life here in Vanpore. King Jaskar Dharman has promised you a court position. Why you want to go back? Why do you care?"

"Because it matters," said Tasvak. "Trishala matters."

He was even more determined now.

"Don't you like Vanpore?" asked Sarvadni. "It is the most pious place on earth, with thousands of temples all around."

"The way people here treat cetas and Dhatakis, I think Vanpore is the most godless place on earth," said Tasvak.

"The thousands of beautiful temples here couldn't attract a single god."

Guru Sarvadni was surprised. He had never heard Tasvak speak with such conviction.

"And I hate the fact that I can't do anything about it," Tasvak added. "If I get power, then maybe I can."

"You have matured so much in the past year," said Sarvadni. He was very proud.

Tasvak didn't say anything, but Sarvadni knew that he had made up his mind to attack Trishala.

Sarvadni thought for a moment. He then got up, and asked Tasvak to follow him. He led Tasvak to a private room, and closed the door.

"I have a plan," said Sarvadni. "If we do this well, Jaskar Dharman may be persuaded to help you."

As Sarvadni narrated the plan, Tasvak shook his head in disbelief. What Sarvadni was asking was wrong.

"You will not be doing anything wrong, Tasvak," insisted the guru. "My duty in this life is complete. I have been thinking of fasting until death, just like my guru, and others before me."

Tasvak was listening.

"But doing what I say gives me an opportunity to die for a cause instead," Sarvadni continued. "Don't deny me this opportunity, Tasvak. Think of this as a final tribute to your teacher."

Tasvak was too stunned to react. Tears in his eyes, he opened the door and walked out.

As he walked home with Avani, Tasvak was lost in his

thoughts. He kept thinking of Guru Sarvadni, and what he had asked him to do.

The whole idea seemed wrong, even sinful. Sarvadni had been more than a father to him. He had even saved his life. Also, there was no guarantee that Jaskar Dharman would help even after Tasvak carried out Sarvadni's plan.

But, then, Sarvadni himself was insisting that it was the right thing to do. Tasvak agreed that this plan was the only chance he had. It was also the only chance Trishala had for getting rid of Nahusha and the Rongchas. Didn't the end justify the means?

Tasvak thought of discussing with Avani. But like him, she was too involved. She owed Sarvadni her life, just as he did – after all, he could save her life only because Sarvadni saved his.

He needed objective, unemotional advice. After giving some thought, he decided to approach Viraj, the only other person he could trust.

"If you don't go ahead, nothing changes," said Viraj. "But if you go ahead, there is a chance that things will change for the better."

Viraj's simple reasoning made things much clearer.

"Also," Viraj added, "if Sarvadni wants to die anyway, then where is the guilt coming from?"

Tasvak nodded in agreement. He had made his decision.

37

GURU SARVADNI

"For everyone else, home is the sweetest place in the world," said Prince Jivak. "But for me, it is the scariest. Because it is where my father lives – my evil father, who killed my loving wife and innocent son. My life is unbearable, Guru Sarvadni."

Guru Sarvadni had invited Prince Jivak for counseling that evening. Jivak had been depressed ever since he was brought back from Khara by Jaskar Dharman.

"You shouldn't think like that," said Sarvadni. "Life is a river, so just go with its flow. You will find your peace and salvation."

"My life is a puddle, there is no flow," replied Jivak, wiping his tears.

"Close your eyes and relax, my prince," said Guru Sarvadni. "Try to avoid the disturbing thoughts, and calm your mind."

They both closed their eyes, and sat still in meditation. Suddenly, the lone lamp went off, and there was darkness. In that darkness, two shadows entered.

"Never dare to go against King Nahusha." one of them shouted.

Jivak fumbled for his sword. But before he could do anything, he heard Guru Sarvadni mumble "Sarvabhu!". As he turned around, something hard hit his head. He was knocked out immediately.

When Jivak regained his conscious, he saw his father Jaskar Dharman and brother Yashthi.

"Where is Guru Sarvadni?" Jivak asked.

"He is dead," replied Yashthi. "Stabbed in the heart. You are lucky to be alive."

"My wife, my son, and now my guru – all are dead," sobbed Jivak. "I hate you, father."

Jaskar Dharman had no patience for Jivak, but he remained calm.

"If you are not happy with your life, then hate your life, not me," said the king. "But answer me first. Do you have any idea who those attackers were?"

"They were assassins sent by Nahusha," said Jivak. "I don't know what you did to Nahusha, but Guru Sarvadni has paid the price with his life."

"Now, leave me alone," he added, turning his head away.

38

THE PUPPET

King Jaskar Dharman had been meditating since he came back from the cremation. He had not spoken much since Sarvadni's killing. The expression on his face was unperturbed, but one could see glimpses of the anger within.

Guru Sarvadni had been killed under his watch. His son was left for dead. This was an assault on Yashantika, and Nahusha was not going to get away with it.

Jaskar Dharman opened his eyes, stood up, and bowed to Sarvabhu. He then called for Viraj.

"Tell your friend to meet me immediately," Jaskar Dharman ordered Viraj.

Tasvak was ready. Guru Sarvadni had expected this meeting to happen soon after his death.

"My condolences, Prince Tasvak," said the king, as Tasvak appeared before him.

"Guru Sarvadni had warned me that this could happen," said Jaskar Dharman. "He had mentioned that with the Rongchas supporting him, Nahusha now has delusion of being more powerful than me. I should have listened to him."

Tasvak nodded.

"But this is not the time for grief," continued Jaskar Dharman. "I will get the army ready. We need to attack immediately, and catch Nahusha by surprise. Otherwise, he will seek reinforcements from Igati."

"I agree," said Tasvak.

"I will send a troop of five hundred soldiers," said Jaskar Dharman. "They can take Trishala easily."

"There are around three hundred Rongcha soldiers in Trishala," said Tasvak. "Rongchas are brave fighters, and they will put up a strong resistance if you attack them head on."

"I have thought about that," countered the king. "The troop will include a hundred Dhatakis. The Dhatakis will lead the attack, and damage the Rongcha barriers before the rest of the troop strikes."

The Dhatakis enrolled in Yashantika's army for the honor of becoming martyrs. They were told that if they die bravely in the battlefield, the sins of their past lives will be cleansed, and they will be born as grahavars in their next life.

"Taking Trishala after the Rongchas are eliminated will be child's play," continued Jaskar Dharman. "The troops will burn Trishala, and bring Nahusha to his knees."

Tasvak's aim was to dethrone Nahusha, and force Rongchas to leave Trishala. Burning Trishala for that was not acceptable. Tasvak was also concerned about throwing away the Dhataki lives, but he thought against bringing that up at the moment.

"I am concerned about the large number of lives being lost," said Tasvak.

"Trishala is our enemy," said Jaskar Dharman. "Don't sympathize with the enemy, or it will cost you a war."

"Our enemy is Nahusha, and the Rongchas who support him," said Tasvak. "Trishala is already a city under siege, and I know that the people of Trishala don't support the Rongchas. In fact, they will readily support us in getting rid of the Rongchas."

"What do you suggest?" asked Jaskar Dharman. He was not used to his plans being challenged, especially by someone as inexperienced as Tasvak.

"I have observed the Rongchas closely while I was at Trishala, and I know their weakness," said Tasvak. "We can play it to our success."

Jaskar Dharman was listening intently.

"If you allow me, I have an alternate plan to capture Nahusha and eliminate the Rongchas," Tasvak offered. "This plan will reduce the chances of damage to Yashantika forces. Also, we need not burn Trishala."

Jaskar Dharman nodded.

"The plan is to lure the Rongchas away from Trishala, and capture Trishala behind their back," said Tasvak.

He then explained his plan in detail.

Jaskar Dharman smiled as he listened. He was impressed with how deeply Tasvak had thought out the details, and how well he was able to exploit his resources, his contacts in Trishala, and his knowledge of the Rongchas to his advantage.

As Tasvak finished, there was just one concern.

"This is a good strategy, except one thing," said the king. "The Idany tribals are extremely hostile to outsiders. Why would they help us?"

"They won't be hostile to us," assured Tasvak. "They have sworn their loyalty to me, and they detest Nahusha. They are on our side in this battle."

Jaskar Dharman nodded in approval.

He called Prince Yashthi, briefed him on the strategy, and asked him to get the troops ready by the next day.

Tasvak was relieved that Guru Sarvadni's death had not been in vain.

"I am grateful for this help," said Tasvak, as he rose to leave.

"I am glad you are," said Jaskar Dharman. "We agree, then, that as a token of this gratitude, Trishala will double its tribute to Yashantika when you become the king."

Tasvak was taken by surprise. He knew that he was being exploited, but he was not in a position to negotiate.

"As you wish," said Tasvak. He bowed to the king, and left.

When they were alone, Prince Yashthi looked at his father.

"Father, are you making him the king of Trishala?" asked Yashthi.

"Yes, my son," said Jaskar Dharman. "After we win the battle, we will dethrone Nahusha and make Tasvak the king."

"I don't understand," said Yashthi. "Why?"

"We all know that Nahusha is Rongcha's puppet," explained Jaskar Dharman. "So, his actions must have Rongcha's blessings."

Yashthi nodded.

"Nahusha sending assassins to Vanpore indicates that Rongchas are now getting delusional about their power," continued Jaskar Dharman. "If this continues, they may annex Trishala any day."

"We can't let that happen!" exclaimed Yashthi.

"Yes, my son, we can't let that happen," said Jaskar Dharman. "So, we need to remove Rongcha's puppet from Trishala's throne, and install our own."

"Tasvak is our puppet," said Yashthi.

"Yes," said Jaskar Dharman. "He is lowborn and inexperienced, and has been bullied all his life – he will be very easy to control. Didn't you see how readily he agreed to double the tribute?"

"He didn't have much of a choice now, father," said Yashthi. "But what if, after gaining power, he doesn't listen to us?"

"Then we can always remove him," replied Jaskar Dharman.

39

THE BATTLE FOR TRISHALA

The Rongcha troops rejoiced when they saw only about a hundred Yashantika soldiers assembled on the opposite bank of river Girika.

They were expecting to meet a much larger army when they left Trishala, and had gathered all their force in Trishala for the combat, leaving Kindisha and the Trishala army to defend the city. But now, it looked like they shouldn't have bothered. They outnumbered the Yashantika troops three to one.

They waited for the Yashantika troops to cross the Trishala bridge, and come to their side. But the Yashantika troops did not move. Instead, the Rongchas could see the Yashantika soldiers across the river mocking them.

Rongchas were not known to be the most patient of people. But they waited for a day, and then another. Finally, on the third day, they couldn't find a good reason to wait any longer, and decided to cross the bridge themselves.

The Yashantika soldiers saw the Rongchas coming, and got into action. They engaged with the Rongchas initially, and then started receding.

The Rongchas were elated. But they did not want to leave the Yashantika forces, who had threatened and mocked them, so cheaply. They wanted to hand out a thrashing Yashantika will remember for years to come. So, they kept pursuing the receding Yashantika troops further inwards.

All of a sudden, additional troops of Yashantika soldiers appeared from nowhere, and surrounded the Rongchas on three sides. The Rongchas had been led into a trap – they had followed a bait, and were now standing against a much larger army.

The Rongchas panicked. With Yashantika soldiers approaching them from three sides, the only option for them was to retreat. They turned around, and ran for the bridge. But as they reached the bridge, they found that it was up in flames. Somebody had put the wooden bridge on fire.

Cornered, the Rongchas had no option left but to fight. The soldiers fought bravely, but were no match for the Yashantika forces.

Tasvak's plan had worked. Trishala was now free of the Rongchas.

Tasvak, with a hundred soldiers, had split from the

rest of the Yashantika army, and crossed the Girika river at the Idany settlement. After a warm reunion with Chief Bhura, he reminded Bhura of his promise of support. Chief Bhura, true to his word, provided Tasvak with fifty of his best warriors.

Tasvak and his troop moved ahead quietly. They took position near the Trishala bridge, and waited. When the Rongcha forces were lured across by the Yashantika soldiers, the Idany warriors worked their way to the bridge, unnoticed because of their camouflage, and set it on fire.

Having eliminated the Rongchas, Tasvak and his troop now moved towards Trishala, and attacked the Trishala army led by Prince Kindisha.

Kindisha was baffled on seeing Tasvak. He had not expected him or the Yashantika troops to get past the Rongchas. He fought, but soon realized that the battle was a lost cause. Abandoning his troops, he escaped into the city, rushed to the upper town, and closed the gates. Nahusha had already dispatched a message to Igati asking for help, and it was only a matter of a day or two before the Rongcha reinforcements arrived.

Most of the Trishala soldiers refused to fight against Tasvak. The others were better traders than fighters. When Kindisha abandoned them, they were convinced of their defeat, and fled.

Tasvak entered Trishala and took control of the lower town. The people rejoiced to learn that their prince Tasvak had returned to Trishala, and that he had chased the Rongchas away.

Meanwhile, Prince Yashthi reached Trishala, and joined Tasvak.

Celebrating the win, Yashthi ordered his soldiers to loot Trishala's lower town. Tasvak opposed him strongly.

"These are my soldiers," said Yashthi, taking exception. "They will not listen to you. They have fought well, and deserve their reward."

"I agree with you, Prince Yashthi," said Tasvak, politely. "But I think that it will be unwise to loot and burn Trishala. If you do so, I won't be able to collect the tribute for Yashantika. Your father will be very unhappy if that happens."

Fearing his father's anger, Prince Yashthi agreed.

Meanwhile, in the upper town, Princess Keya and Minister Kathik were following the developments closely. Now that the Rongchas were out, they could see that the general mood of the people was against Nahusha and Kindisha.

They called a meeting of the nobles, and convinced them that resisting Tasvak did not make sense anymore. The nobles unanimously decided to open the gates.

Keya and Kathik, with the nobles behind them, warmly welcomed Tasvak as he stepped into the palace.

Tasvak went straight to Nahusha's bedchamber. Nahusha was getting ready for the battle, and Kindisha was sitting by his side.

"There is no need for you to get ready, brother," said Tasvak. "The battle is already over."

Before Nahusha and Kindisha could react, Tasvak's

soldiers arrested them.

"You are not fit to rule," said Nahusha. "You son of a mlechcha, you will ruin this kingdom."

"Ruin this kingdom?" said Tasvak. "What is left to ruin? You have done all the damage already."

"You always wanted the throne," said Kindisha.

"No, brother," said Tasvak. "I tried playing by your rules. And do you know what I found? It doesn't work."

"I trusted you," said Nahusha. "I made you my emissary."

"Yes, you did," responded Tasvak "You made me an emissary and sent me to fight the Idany tribals, in the hope that they will kill me."

"I was happy working under you, did all that you asked me to," he continued. "What was the result? You betrayed me, and then sentenced me to death."

He stared at his brothers for a moment. It was time to let go of the emotions and do the right thing.

"Take them to the elephant house, and have the elephants trample them," he ordered the soldiers.

Nahusha and Kindisha were stunned. They never knew that Tasvak was capable of sentencing them to death.

"Forgive me, brother, I was wrong," pleaded Nahusha, with the fear of death in his eyes. "It was Kindisha who asked me to have you killed."

Tasvak looked at Nahusha with disgust.

"You have a choice, my brother," cried Nahusha. "Spare me!"

"Yes, I have a choice," said Tasvak. "And it is between you and me."

"If I have to choose between you and me, it is always going to be me," he added, and walked out.

40

THE RETURN OF TASVAK

"As your king, I will work towards bringing peace, harmony, and prosperity back to Trishala," Tasvak vowed solemnly, standing before the nobles of Trishala after his coronation.

He had taken the reins of a kingdom that had been under siege for almost two years. Looting by the Rongchas and the excessive tributes it had been forced to pay had left Trishala weak and poor, a mere shadow of the glorious kingdom in his father's reign.

He was in the council room, with Queen Avani, Princess Keya and Viraj by his side. The nobles, led by Minister Kathik, were seated before him. These nobles had served his father, then Nahusha after him, and had allied with the Rongchas when they controlled Trishala. Till a few days back, many of them had considered Tasvak a fugitive, and an enemy of Trishala.

As Tasvak looked around, he could see the fear on the noble's faces. He knew what they were thinking. Keya had informed him earlier about their concerns.

"We are worried about our future, even about our life," Kathik had told Princess Keya. "The man killed his brothers without a second thought, why will he spare us?"

This was the time to put such apprehensions to rest.

"This is a new beginning for all of us," said Tasvak. "Even those who fought against me have nothing to worry about, as long as they stay loyal to me."

He looked around once again. This time, he saw that the fear had subsided somewhat.

"But, from now on, you need to be very careful," he added, sternly. "If you even think of going against me, the consequences will be severe. I will not only sentence you to death, but also imprison your family, and confiscate your wealth."

The nobles took the hint, and one after the other declared their fulsome support and undying loyalty to their beloved king.

With the nobles firmly in his control, King Tasvak's next task was to gain the confidence of the people of Trishala.

Although the people appreciated that Tasvak had freed Trishala of the Rongchas, they did not see Tasvak as a compassionate ruler. That he was the ugly son of a mlechcha mother, a monster who had mercilessly killed his stepbrothers, did not work in his favor.

Tasvak needed the help of someone who believed in him, and who could convince the people to change their views. He thought of Trivit, the charismatic monk who he knew from his stay at Vakshi, and called him to Trishala.

Trivit arrived in Trishala with a few of his followers. He was very glad to see that Tasvak had been successful in his quest for the throne of Trishala.

"The nobles have accepted me as their king," Tasvak told Trivit. "But I am not sure about the common people. I am always afraid that they will revolt against me."

"People revolt only when they are pushed to a wall," said Trivit. "Gain the support of the downtrodden, the disadvantaged, and those who have faced setbacks in life – and you will never face an uprising."

"I have every intention to do so," said Tasvak. "But the people hate me. They think that I am a sinner because I killed my stepbrothers."

"They will come around," smiled Trivit. "Power makes people ignore your sins. There is not much difference between acquiring power and achieving sainthood."

Trivit's followers reached out to the people of Trishala. They eloquently praised the new king, told stories about Tasvak's bravery, his hardships, and convinced their listeners about Tasvak's commitment to the betterment of the kingdom. It did not take long before Tasvak gained acceptance among the people.

Tasvak had finally achieved what he had set out to do when he left Vakshi. He missed Guru Sarvadni, but he was glad that he had Trivit to guide him in Sarvadni's absence.

41

A Way of Life

Ajabuhi had come a long way since Tasvak last met Trivit in Vakshi. It now had more than a handful of dedicated followers.

Tasvak's request to reach out to the masses appealed to Trivit, as not only did it help propagate Tasvak's message, but also gave his followers a chance to tell people about Ajabuhi.

"Ajabuhi is not a religion," people were told. "It is a way of life."

For the people who felt constrained by the strict, and sometimes regressive, morality of Tapasi, Ajabuhi came as a welcome change.

Viraj was the first in Trishala to join Ajabuhi.

"In Tapasi, they tell you not to kill a man because it is a sin," Viraj told Tasvak. "So, as an assassin, I have no hope for salvation in Tapasi. But in Ajabuhi, they ask why do you want to kill a man, and judge you based on your motive."

He had found acceptance in Ajabuhi.

Tapasi was an old religion, which had not changed much for centuries. It forced the scriptures, written ages ago, in another era.

In contrast, Ajabuhi had a more progressive outlook. It said "Knowledge is important. Pursue it, but do not hold on to bygone knowledge in scriptures. If it is forgotten, it was not required. If it is required, it cannot be forgotten."

This appealed to the younger people, who appreciated Ajabuhi's ability to forget the past, and adapt to the new.

But the most important aspect of Ajabuhi was the way it released people from the shackles of their birth.

Tapasi said "Sarvabhu decides what role we are going to play in this life." Traditionally, that role was decided by the person's birth.

Ajabuhi put the onus on the individual, saying "We decide what role we will play. We will be judged by our deeds, not by our birth."

This appealed to the lowborns, who now were no longer limited by the roles assigned to them by traditions.

Similarly, while Tapasi subdued women, Ajabuhi empowered them if they became monks.

Tapasi said "An unmarried woman is the property of her father, and in absence of her father, her brother. Once married, she becomes the property of her husband. On her husband's death, she must immolate herself in his pyre."

Ajabuhi said "A women is property of her father, brother or husband. But once she declares herself an Ajabuhi monk, she is free."

Ajabuhi further eliminated the practice of widow immolation. This lead to scores of repressed women taking up Ajabuhi.

Trivit's followers reached out to the people, and organized prayer meetings all over Trishala. In these meetings, they talked about the tenets of Ajabuhi, and how it presented a better way to lead lives.

Soon, Ajabuhi had gained significant following among the people of Trishala.

Ajabuhi also had King Tasvak's strong support. Tasvak encouraged people in Trishala, commoners as well as nobles, to follow Ajabuhi practices. He donated land and funded Ajabuhi to set up a monastery in the region.

Tasvak remembered Guru Sarvadni's words about Trishala someday getting a king who is not afraid to confront the past. As he backed Ajabuhi, Tasvak felt proud of being that king.

42

THE MONK AND THE
PRINCESS

"The Ajabuhi monk, Trivit, is here to meet you," announced the guard.

"Show him in," said Princess Keya.

She had been expecting this meeting ever since she had stopped Trishala's aid to the Ajabuhi monastery. She had convinced King Tasvak to let her do so due to shortage of funds in the treasury.

"Honoring your promise to Yashantika, we have doubled their tribute," she had told Tasvak. "But this means that we cannot afford to give aid to the Ajabuhi monastery."

Tasvak had reluctantly agreed.

"Welcome," Keya smiled politely, as Trivit walked in.

"How can I help the mighty high monk of Ajabuhi?"

"You give undue credit to this feeble human," said Trivit, as he sat down.

There was silence as Princess Keya waited for Trivit to speak.

"The Ajabuhi monastery is facing some problems since you stopped the aid," said Trivit.

"Trishala's treasury is currently running short," said Keya. "We can't afford to fund religious establishments at this time."

"I understand," said Trivit. "But the aid to Tapasi monasteries has not been suspended."

"Ajabuhi is not Tapasi," scoffed Keya. "Tapasi has been in Trishala since before anyone can remember. Trishala has honored its commitments to the Tapasi monasteries for centuries."

"Ajabuhi is not a religion," said Trivit. "It is a way of life. Unlike Tapasi, it empowers people, especially women, to deal with the hardships in their lives. You are welcome to visit our monastery to understand it better."

"I know how to deal with hardships in my life." Keya sounded offended. "Men like you can never truly understand the hardships faced by women. A man advising a woman on handling her troubles is like a person with twisted ankle advising a person with broken leg on how to walk."

"You speak the truth, princess." Trivit decided that it was better to retreat. "Women face far more problems than men in their life."

An awkward silence followed.

"Still, if there is anything the Ajabuhi monastery can do for the kingdom," offered Trivit, as he stood up to leave, "or for you personally, you only have to ask."

"Thank you, but you can't do anything," Keya said, concluding the discussion. "The aid to Ajabuhi will resume when the finances of Trishala are back on track."

Trivit waited for a moment, then bowed and took her leave. As he smiled at her, Princess Keya didn't fail to notice a tiny crease on his forehead.

43

THE QUEEN IN WAITING

Trishala was changing. A number of things were happening all around. But in all this, one person remained in the background – Avani.

Avani had never aspired to become a queen. She was just another girl in the lower town when fate intervened. And now, as the queen of King Tasvak of Trishala, she found herself trying hard to fit in her new surroundings. She changed her hair, her dressing style, and even her mannerisms to match those of the noble ladies of the court. But no matter what she tried, she still felt like an outsider.

With Tasvak busy building a new Trishala, Avani looked at Princess Keya for support. Avani had always been in awe of Princess Keya. But, pretending to be her friend, Keya took every opportunity to undermine an unsuspecting Avani.

"People might not like seeing a commoner on the throne," Keya told her, when Avani mentioned that she was interested in attending the court. "It's better that you stay away for now. Once everything settles down, I will invite you myself."

Avani kept waiting, but that invitation never arrived. The nobles took her absence from the court as a sign of the king's displeasure towards her.

In time, Avani felt ignored and sidelined by Tasvak. She was unhappy and depressed, but Tasvak never noticed. He was overwhelmed with his work. The unhappiness Avani felt everyday made her question her relationship with Tasvak, and she approached Trivit for advice.

"What is a good relationship?" she asked Trivit. "What is the worth of a relationship that causes one to be unhappy?"

"A good relationship is not a refuge from your problems, but an oasis where you can grow better as person," said Trivit, sympathetically. "No relationship is worth your sorrow."

However, as the Varti festival approached, Avani almost forgot her sorrows. She had missed Varti while in Vanpore, and was excited about the grand celebrations in the palace. She shared her excitement with Princess Keya.

"Did you get a formal invitation from the king?" Keya asked.

Avani was confused.

"No, I didn't," she said.

"That means the king doesn't need you," said Keya. "Perhaps he doesn't want to be seen with you publicly. So, don't embarrass him. Stay in your chambers."

"But I am the queen," said Avani. "Will I not be needed in the rituals?"

"You are a commoner, Avani, who is married to the King," scoffed Keya. "You can't be a real queen. Your role in King Tasvak's life is over. Soon, he will marry a noble girl. The faster you learn your true place, the better it will be for you."

The news of Tasvak marrying again left Avani heart-broken. Tasvak hadn't even cared to inform her. Tears rolling on her face, she remembered Trivit's advice, "No relation is worth your sorrow."

That evening, Tasvak was shocked to see Avani getting ready to leave the palace.

"Where are you going?" asked Tasvak.

"I am going away," said Avani.

"Why? What is wrong? Why are you behaving this way?"

Tasvak was unable to comprehend what was happening.

"What I have done wrong?" sobbed Avani. "I did whatever you wanted me to do. You said let us go to Vakshi, I followed you. You said let us get married, I did. You said let us go to Vanpore, I did."

"Yes, and I respect you for that," said Tasvak. He was still confused.

"You called me here," said Avani, looking at Tasvak. "I

was not allowed to accompany you to the court, because I might embarrass you. I stayed hidden, always scared of doing something wrong."

She looked at Tasvak for a moment. He was staring at her blankly.

"Now you want to marry a noble girl, who will be more suitable as a queen. You can, but I don't want to be here to see it."

"I am not marrying anyone," said Tasvak. He was wondering who could have put this idea in Avani's mind.

"I had no idea that you were so unhappy," he said. "Why didn't you tell me?"

"You didn't even notice," cried Avani. "You don't care about me anymore. You don't need me. I am leaving you to become an Ajabuhi monk."

"Avani, stop," Tasvak pleaded. "Nothing that you just said is true."

"This is not my imagination," said Avani, her voice choking with emotion. "The humiliation I face everyday is real."

"I am sorry, Avani," said Tasvak, holding her hand.

"I am going away," she said, breaking into tears. "Now you won't be embarrassed by me. Now you won't have to hide me."

"Avani, you are my strength, my pride," said Tasvak. "Why would I want to hide you? A person wants to hide his weakness, not his strength."

Avani was surprised.

"But aren't you embarrassed by me?" she asked. "Aren't

you embarrassed by my looks, my color, my being a commoner."

"You are beautiful, and you know that," smiled Tasvak. "You just want to hear it from me."

He moved closer to Avani.

"You know what makes me really happy?" he asked.

"What?" asked Avani, looking at Tasvak.

"You!" whispered Tasvak.

"Now you are lying," said Avani, wiping her tears.

"No, I am not," said Tasvak. "In fact, I hate loving you so much. It makes me vulnerable."

"Then don't," said Avani.

"How can I not?" asked Tasvak, looking into Avani's eyes. "You remind me of the goodness in me."

They both stared at each other in silence. Avani smiled.

"Then why didn't I get invited to the Varti celebrations?" she asked.

Tasvak was surprised.

"Why do you need to be invited?" he asked. "You are the queen, the hostess of the celebrations. You are the one who invites the guests."

Avani considered that for a moment, then smiled sheepishly. She felt silly for being so easily manipulated by Princess Keya.

"I see now," she said. "I guess I was overwhelmed by our reality. I forgot that we are a normal couple."

"We are not normal, and will never be normal," smiled Tasvak. "Our story is an epic – epic failure or epic success, but an epic story nonetheless."

Next day, Keya was surprised to see Avani in the court with Tasvak.

"The people of Trishala will not approve," advised Keya.

"I will worry about the people," retorted Tasvak. "But tell me, sister, do you approve of Avani as a queen?"

"She is a good person, but not fit to be the queen," said Keya. "She is weak. You need a strong, noble girl as your wife."

"The person you are calling weak is my rock," said Tasvak, his displeasure apparent in his voice. "She is one of the strongest persons I have ever met, and she is the only person I will ever call my wife."

Keya smiled, looked at Avani, and walked away. Her plan to subdue Avani had failed miserably.

44

SKELETONS IN THE CLOSET

Minister Kathik was watching Trivit's growing influence helplessly. When he and Princess Keya helped Tasvak take the throne, they had thought that they will be able to control the inexperienced Tasvak.

Tasvak was being controlled, but not by them. He was under the influence of a devious monk and his new faith. An ardent Tapasi follower, Kathik hated Ajabuhi, he hated Trivit, and he hated Trivit's control over Tasvak.

But now, things were going to change. He had heard a rumor that, if true, would weaken Ajabuhi. And if Ajabuhi weakened, so would Trivit.

He was eager to share the news with Keya. He tried reaching her at the Varti celebrations, but changed his mind when he saw her responding favorably to Viraj's advances.

After the celebrations, Keya approached him, and they walked to the palace under the pretense of official work.

"Did you inform King Jaskar Dharman about the growth of Ajabuhi in Trishala?" Keya asked Kathik.

"Yes, I had sent an urgent request for help to Jaskar Dharman," answered Kathik. "But because of the huge tribute our king pays to Yashantika, he refused to get involved."

This was disappointing news. Keya had hoped that Jaskar Dharman, a devout Tapasi follower, would force Tasvak to remove Ajabuhi from Trishala.

"We can't let Ajabuhi take over Trishala," Keya said. "We need to stop Trivit."

"There have been some other developments," said Kathik. "I have heard a rumor. But I can't speak openly, it will be my head if the word gets out."

"You don't have to worry about me," assured Keya. "As you know, I am not close to anyone in Trishala."

He wanted to believe Keya, but her exchanges earlier in the day with Viraj made him cautious. Viraj was an Ajabuhi follower, and a close adviser to King Tasvak.

"Not even Viraj?" asked Kathik, stroking his beard.

"You speak very freely, minister." Keya was offended, but realized that Kathik's caution was justified on his part. "But you shouldn't worry, it's part of the plan."

"Viraj thinks that I am a victim, and fancies himself as my protector," she explained. "He can provide me information that may be useful to us."

Kathik nodded.

"Princess, you are such a strong person," he said. "Why do you always have to play the victim?"

Keya laughed.

"My stepbrother Kindisha acted very strong," she replied. "Look where he is now. I would rather play the victim than be one."

Kathik smiled. They had a lot in common.

"Now, speak up," said Keya. "What is the rumor?"

"There has been talk about Ajabuhi monks exploiting their female followers," whispered Kathik. "There was a rumor about an incident a few weeks back, but it was hushed up."

"Is there any evidence?" asked Keya. After Trivit's claims the other day about Ajabuhi empowering women, this was rather unexpected.

"No, at this point this is just a rumor," said Kathik. "But certainly, there are skeletons in the closet. I will keep my eyes open for any new incidents."

45

GOOD RIDDANCE

Princess Keya found an opportunity to speak against Ajabuhi sooner than expected.

Just a few days later, Keya's chambermaid came to her, pleading for help.

"Princess, save me!" she said, breathlessly. "Please save me, or they will kill me."

"What happened?" asked Keya, "Who is trying to kill you?"

"The Ajabuhi monk attacked me," the maid sobbed. "He tried to take advantage of me."

Keya asked her to tell the incident in detail.

"My husband is an Ajabuhi follower," the maid said. "Over the past few months, he has been going to the Ajabuhi monastery. Today, he took me along, and asked me to meet the monk Stoka."

The maid burst into tears. Keya consoled her, and asked her to continue.

"When I entered Stoka's chamber, he attacked me," the maid continued in a trembling voice. "As I pushed him away and ran out, he threatened that nobody can save me – that there will be consequences if I tell anybody."

Keya had known the maid since her childhood. She remembered what Kathik had told her, but had not imagined that her own maid could be a victim. She was furious.

She immediately took the maid to King Tasvak, and told him about the incident.

"I will investigate this incident myself," Tasvak assured Keya.

"With your permission, I would like to accompany you," said Keya. "I want to see how monk Trivit responds to these accusations."

Tasvak agreed reluctantly. He still remembered Keya's treatment of Avani, and wondered if this was another of her manipulations.

On reaching the Ajabuhi monastery, Tasvak met Trivit and told him about the accusation.

Trivit called Stoka, and asked him about the incident. Stoka appeared shocked at the accusation, and declined outright.

"I don't know why the maid is lying," said Stoka.

"She is not lying," Keya objected. "I know her since her childhood. She will never make up such stories."

"If she is not making up stories, then maybe you are,"

said Stoka.

"My king, how can you allow this person to talk to your sister like this," fumed Keya. "Our father would have chopped his tongue, here and now."

"I am not my father," said Tasvak, sternly. It was clear that he did not believe Keya.

Keya was beside herself with anger.

"These people are lying," shouted Keya. "They are hypocrites. They are collecting money, abusing women, and you are too feeble to stop them."

"Princess Keya, I beg you," said Trivit, politely. "Please don't insult King Tasvak like this."

"Drop your act, you hypocrite," Keya shot back. "You are a worthless worm, a power hungry monster."

Tasvak didn't like the way Keya was talking to Trivit.

"Don't speak another word, sister," said Tasvak. "Enough of your arrogance, and your lies. Guru Trivit neither needs our money, nor power. He is working for the well-being of the people."

"He is a hypocrite, and a fraud," Keya shouted in humiliation. "And you are a fool not to see it."

"Leave now," ordered Tasvak. "You are not in control of your emotions."

"You don't deserve to be the king, Tasvak," shouted Keya, her face flushed with anger. "You are weaker than Nahusha. I wish you die the way he did."

Keya realized that she had overstepped a boundary. She composed herself, bowed to Tasvak, and walked out.

"I am sorry about the misunderstanding," said Tasvak,

turning towards Trivit.

"It is not my place to speak," replied Trivit.

"Guru Trivit is too modest," said Stoka. "But I can speak if you permit, my king."

"Speak," said Tasvak.

Stoka looked at Trivit, who nodded.

"Princess Keya resents Ajabuhi's popularity, and our guru Trivit's growing influence," said Stoka. "So, first she asked you to suspend the funding to our monastery. Since that didn't discourage us, she is now making up these stories to defame Ajabuhi."

"The funding was stopped temporarily because the treasury was short of funds," said Tasvak. "This is a misunderstanding."

"Perhaps, my king," said Stoka, with deference. "But she is not only after us. She is after you as well. As you just heard, Princess Keya thinks that you don't deserve to be the king, and you know that she despises the fact that you married a commoner."

Tasvak was listening.

"After this, my king, I fear for your life," Stoka continued. "There are rumors that she is thinking of assassinating you."

"That's enough!" said Tasvak, and left.

He knew that Keya was headstrong, and was sometimes manipulative. There was never a loving bond between them, but she did help Tasvak gain the trust of Trishala's nobles after he became the king. Tasvak refused to believe that Keya will stoop low enough to plan his assassination.

That night, Tasvak was attacked by an unknown assailant. Though the attack was foiled by his bodyguards, it shattered his trust in Keya.

Next morning, Tasvak called Keya to his palace. Keya was still upset and did not take the matter seriously. But when she noticed that Trivit was also present, she realized that something was wrong.

"Sister, I see that the matters of state are too tiring for you," Tasvak said, kindly. "It is best for you to join the Ajabuhi monastery as a monk, and spend time in the service of people."

"I don't want to be a monk," protested Keya. "I don't even like Ajabuhi."

"The monastery is in Vakshi, far away from Trishala," said Trivit. "You will be safe there. As you know, many people don't like your presence here in Trishala."

"You are removing me from Trishala because I spoke against you," she scoffed, looking at Trivit.

Then she turned towards Tasvak.

"Brother, do you really think I planned that attack on you?" asked Keya. "You know me since childhood. You know that I am not capable of doing such a thing."

"I know what you are capable of, sister," said Tasvak. "Since childhood, I kept tolerating your actions in the hope that you will change. But you didn't change."

"This is no different than the death sentence for me," said Keya.

Tasvak shook his head.

"Everybody dies, but some spend a whole life digging their own grave," he said. "You are one of them. It is too late now, I have taken the decision."

Keya was desperate.

"Please, brother!" she pleaded. "Please don't do this. Please!"

But Tasvak was not listening to her anymore. He ordered the guards to take her away and hand her over to the Ajabuhi monks.

46

THE GRANDSON

"You need to hire bodyguards, my king," said Trivit.

He was concerned due to the recent assassination attempt on Tasvak.

"I already have bodyguards," said Tasvak.

"Not these bodyguards," said Trivit. "You need bodyguards who are so fearsome that an attacker will think a hundred times before targeting you. Deterrence is the key here."

"Where am I going to get such bodyguards?" asked Tasvak.

"In the Kahalava pass," replied Trivit. "The Lokharos."

"But why will the Lokharos serve me?" Tasvak asked. "I have heard that they are too proud to work for anybody."

"They will serve you," assured Trivit. "Not as the king of Trishala, but as the grandson of their chief, the mighty

Zirosthi."

Tasvak could not understand what Trivit was talking about. He looked at Trivit in disbelief.

"Are you humoring me, monk?" he asked. "What makes you think that I am Zirosthi's grandson?"

"It is the truth," smiled Trivit. "I have known that since I first met you in Vakshi. You look so much like Zirosthi."

He looked at Tasvak, who was having a hard time coming to grips with this surprising revelation.

"If you remember, I once told you that I was captured by Lokharos," said Trivit. "They released me because I promised Zirosthi something."

Tasvak nodded. He could recall their conversation in Vakshi.

"I promised Zirosthi that I will send his grandson to him," said Tasvak.

Tasvak took a moment to respond. He was choked with emotion.

"You scare me sometimes, monk," said Tasvak, as he composed himself. "It looks like you plan everything ahead in time."

"That I do," said Trivit, with a mischievous smile.

47

FEAR AND RESPECT

Tasvak couldn't wait to meet Zirosthi. The messenger he had sent to the Lokharos had brought back an invitation, and it confirmed that Zirosthi was indeed his grandfather. As soon as he could, he put Trishala in the care of Avani, took a few soldiers, and left for the Kahalava pass.

After reaching the Kahalava pass, as he and his soldiers headed for the Lokharo caves, a group of Lokharos appeared from nowhere and gathered around them. He asked his soldiers to turn back to Trishala, and let the Lokharos lead him to their chief.

Tasvak was a giant man, and was used to towering over others. But standing in front of Zirosthi, he felt dwarfed.

Zirosthi stared silently at Tasvak for a long while. The resemblance between their faces was striking, even though Zirosthi's was covered in wrinkles and a long white beard.

"How old are you?" Zirosthi asked, finally.

"I am twenty one," Tasvak answered.

Zirosthi stepped closer.

"You are nothing like your mother," declared Zirosthi.

"I don't know how my mother looked," said Tasvak. "I might have different looks than hers."

Zirosthi smiled.

"You are different because you are alive and she is not," he said. "You know how to survive and she didn't."

Tasvak stayed silent. He was wondering about his mother.

"She was a naive young girl," Zirosthi continued. "She fell in love with your father when he was here for pilgrimage. A few months after he went back, she gave birth to you."

He sighed, and looked at Tasvak.

"She thought your father will accept her as a wife and make you a prince. I told her not go. Foolish child, she didn't listen, and went to Trishala with you."

Tasvak was listening intently. Nobody had ever told him anything about his mother.

"When I heard that your father had killed her, I wanted to kill him," he said. "But my men informed me that you are alive, and have been accepted as a prince of Trishala. Killing your father would have taken that away from you, so I let it be."

There was a long silence, and then Zirosthi spoke

again.

"But all that is in the past – why dig up the dead corpses?" he smiled, trying to hide the sad look in his eyes. "Let us talk about you. Why are you here now?"

"To meet you," replied Tasvak.

"Now you have met me," said Zirosthi. "Speak, what do you want from your grandfather?"

Zirosthi was speaking with such authority that Tasvak felt as if he were a young boy, not the king of Trishala.

"I need Lokharos warriors as my bodyguards," said Tasvak.

"Why?" asked Zirosthi.

"I have heard that Lokharos are fearless and loyal fighters," replied Tasvak.

"You have heard right," said Zirosthi. "But why will they be loyal to you?"

"They will be loyal to me if you tell them to," said Tasvak. "You are their leader."

"In what world do you live?" laughed Zirosthi. "I met you just now. If I tell my people to be loyal to you because you are my grandson, I will lose their respect."

Tasvak did not know what to say. He did not like being laughed at.

"So, what should I do to gain loyalty from them?" he asked. "Pay them gold karshikas?"

"You are your mother's son," smiled Zirosthi, shaking his head. "No patience."

Tasvak felt chastised.

"You need to stay here," said Zirosthi. "Train with

them, and handpick the people you trust."

Tasvak nodded.

"You should learn not only their names, but everything about them," Zirosthi continued. "You have to earn their respect and loyalty. You have to prove why, when the time comes, you deserve to live and not them. If you can convince them that you are worthy of their lives, take them with you. Do you agree?"

"I agree," said Tasvak, without any hesitation.

"If they agree to be your bodyguards," said Zirosthi, "I assure you, nobody can ever touch you until the last Lokharo is standing beside you."

Tasvak stayed. After two months, he had picked his troop of trusted bodyguards.

When he was about to leave, Zirosthi offered him a drink.

Tasvak hesitated for a moment.

"Take it," said Zirosthi. "When a Lokharo chief offers you a drink, that means he has accepted you as one of his own."

Tasvak took the drink from Zirosthi.

The Lokharos shouted their blessings in unison.

"May you drink so much that you lose your fear, but not so much that you lose your mind."

"May you eat so much that you gain your strength, but not so much that you lose your shape."

Zirosthi moved forward, and embraced Tasvak.

Tasvak froze for a moment, overwhelmed by emotion. Then, he too embraced Zirosthi.

They stood not as the chief of Lokharos and the king of Trishala, but as a grandfather and a grandson who loved each other dearly.

Tasvak then marched to Trishala with his troop of Lokharo bodyguards.

With their deadly Urumi weapons, tall horses, and feral looks, the Lokharos commanded fear and respect for their master, Tasvak, the king of Trishala.

48

THE FRIENDSHIP

It had been long since Chief Snuhi lost his daughter and grandson. He had lost his wish to live, and had become shadow of his former self.

One day, a Tapasi monk arrived in the Vidari settlement. He was looking for Chief Snuhi, and wanted to convey some good news.

Chief Snuhi did not care about any news, but could not refuse a monk's request.

"Tell me, monk," he said. "What good news do you have for me?"

"I am Rudhata," said the monk. "I have news about your grandson."

"My grandson?" Snuhi said. "This is a mistake. My daughter and grandson were murdered by the monster Jaskar Dharman."

"I am sorry about your daughter's untimely death," said Rudhata. "But your grandson is alive and well."

Chief Snuhi looked at Rudhata in disbelief.

"Jaskar Dharman didn't kill your grandson because he has highborn Tapasi blood," explained Rudhata. "But he didn't want Prince Jivak to get attached to his son. So, he sent the child away."

Snuhi was elated, but slightly skeptical.

"How can I believe that the child is my grandson?" he asked. "He could be an impostor."

"The child has a birthmark on his left foot," replied Rudhata.

Snuhi remembered how his daughter used to fondly show the boy's foot to him, giving it a funny name. This was enough to convince Snuhi.

"Where is he?" he asked, tears of joy in his eyes. "I want to bring him here. Where can I see him?"

"He is with King Tasvak of Trishala," said Rudhata.

Snuhi's face fell.

"Why will King Tasvak return my grandson?" he asked. "He is Jaskar Dharman's ally."

"King Tasvak only recently learned that the child is your grandson," said Rudhata. "He has already arranged to send the child. I am here to give you the news."

"Has my grandson been harmed in any way?" asked Snuhi.

"King Tasvak has taken very good care of the boy," said Rudhata. "The boy was very sick when found, but King Tasvak and his wife saved him."

"I am grateful to King Tasvak," said Snuhi. "Vidaris judge a man's character by how he treats people he does not know, and things he does not own. King Tasvak has taken good care of my grandson, which shows that he is good and trustworthy."

Rudhata smiled. He waited for a moment, then moved on to the other reason he was there.

"If you are willing, King Tasvak would like Vidari and Trishala to be friends," said Rudhata. "He wants have a treaty between the two as a token of the friendship."

"What are the terms of the treaty?" Snuhi asked.

"At present, Vidari sells its produce for a very low price to middlemen, who sell it at a high premium to the traders in Trishala," said Rudhata. "As a result, neither you, nor the traders get the fair price."

"That has always been a problem," said Snuhi. "We don't have a choice because we are not allowed to directly supply our produce in Trishala, and the traders in Trishala find it risky to travel all the way here for our produce."

"The treaty will allow you to supply your produce, at a fair price, directly to traders in Trishala," said Rudhata. "In return, you agree not to sell to anybody else. Your produce will be sold only in Trishala."

Chief Snuhi readily agreed.

His work done, Rudhata went back to Trishala with the good news.

After a few days, Tasvak visited the Vidari settlement with the little boy. Chief Snuhi was overjoyed on seeing his grandson alive. Tasvak and a grateful Snuhi then signed the treaty, and the friendship between Trishala and Vidari was sealed.

As a result of the treaty, Trishala became a center for exotic ivory, pearls, and animal hide. This attracted rich merchants from all over Jivavarta to Trishala. As the trade boomed, Trishala was on the path to greater prosperity.

49

THE POWER OF WEAPONS

Trishala was slowly getting back its former glory. The Rongchas had not came back after their ouster, and Jaskar Dharman was content with the tribute he was getting from Trishala. The treaty with Vidari was paying rich dividends, and Trishala's dark days under the Rongchas were now a distant memory.

Tasvak and Avani became parents to a beautiful boy. Tasvak invited their only family, the Lokharo chief Zirosthi, to come to Trishala and bless them.

Zirosthi was impressed with Trishala's growing prosperity. But he could see something that Tasvak couldn't.

"I see that Trishala's wealth is growing," said Zirosthi, "but not its strength."

"Why does Trishala need strength?" asked Tasvak. "As long as we keep sending the tributes, no one will attack

Trishala."

"Not even the Rongchas?" asked Zirosthi with surprise. "You ousted them from Trishala. Their king Dhanveer does not believe in forgiveness. Also, I wonder if he has forgotten that you killed his son-in-law."

"They should not attack," Tasvak was confident. "At least, not in the near future. Trishala is still giving Rongchas a huge sum in tribute. Although Dhanveer cared for his son-in-law, he cares about his wealth more."

"That might be true for now," smiled Zirosthi. "But what if one day these kingdoms ask you for more than you can give?"

"I have thought about that," said Tasvak. "I am strengthening the army. I am training them well, and have also started recruiting tribals. I realized the power of a well-trained army when I attacked Trishala with the Yashantika soldiers."

"Good," said Zirosthi. "What about the weapons?"

"Trishala imports swords and spears for the army from Yashantika," replied Tasvak.

"What if one day Yashantika refuses to sell you the weapons?" asked Zirosthi.

Tasvak had considered the scenario, but did not have a solution. Trishala did not have any expertise in forging weapons.

"You need to start forging your weapons here in Trishala," said Zirosthi. "And not just spears and swords. Your army is small and inexperienced, so you need more powerful weapons. I will send my weapon master here to teach your people how to make such weapons."

"That will really help, grandfather," said Tasvak, glad that his grandfather was there to guide him.

"Never underestimate the power of weapons," Zirosthi added. "A novice with a powerful weapon is deadlier than a warrior with a stick."

Soon, Trishala started forging its own weapons. With a trained army and an arsenal of its own powerful weapons, it now had no reason to fear Rongcha or Yashantika.

50

ACTS OF KINDNESS

In a short span of time, Ajabuhi had seen a rapid rise in its number of followers. For these followers, Guru Trivit was no less than a god.

Jaskar Dharman had learned about rise of this new faith and its monk from Minister Kathik. At that time, he had ignored it as Trishala's internal matter. But when he heard that the Vidaris were converting to Ajabuhi, he realized that Ajabuhi is an impending threat to Tapasi.

Instead of confronting Tasvak directly, Jaskar Dharman decided to intimidate the Vidaris by increasing the raids on their settlement. As he expected, Chief Snuhi asked Tasvak for help.

Tasvak requested Jaskar Dharman to stop his raids on Vidari. In response, Jaskar Dharman sent Tasvak a stern message.

"I am pained by your request to stop Yashantika's raids on the tribal villages. As rulers of the kingdom, it is our divine duty to keep these savages in check. Instead of helping me in my mission, you chose to side with these savages, and forged an alliance with them. Trishala is advised to stay out of these matters."

Tasvak knew that although Jaskar Dharman justified invading these tribal villages by calling them savages, the real reason was to loot their produce, and acquire cetas. Tasvak thought of confronting Jaskar Dharman, but decided not to. Jaskar Dharman had helped him win Trishala, and he did not want to appear ungrateful.

He decided to ask Trivit for advice on how to help the tribes without directly confronting Jaskar Dharman.

"You could help by funding Ajabuhi monks to rebuild the attacked settlements," suggested Trivit. "That way, these tribes will see you as a compassionate king. You will thus gain their loyalty, and Ajabuhi will get followers."

From then on, whenever the Yashantika troops raided the Vidari settlement, Ajabuhi monks, backed by Tasvak, helped the tribals repair the damages, and take care of the wounded. These acts of kindness persuaded an even larger number of people to join Ajabuhi.

Jaskar Dharman's plan had backfired. He watched helplessly as Ajabuhi slowly displaced Tapasi as the predominant religion in Trishala as well as in the surrounding areas.

51

THE NEPHEW

Soumil had been hearing the story from his mother since his childhood. It was about the fateful day, many years back, when Rongchas soldiers had come looking for him. Just a baby then, he had been chosen for the human sacrifice at the Prahuti festival. She told him how bravely her brother Daras had fought the soldiers, keeping them away, so that they could escape.

They escaped death, but couldn't escape poverty. They settled amidst a small tribal settlement in Khara, where Soumil learned the importance of survival very early in life. He also learned that having money makes survival easy.

At the age of ten, Soumil met a herb trader. He was impressed with the amount of gold karshikas the trader carried, and how luxuriously he lived. So, he decided to become a herb trader himself.

"Will you teach me how to sell herbs?" he asked the trader. "I want to earn money like you."

The trader smiled. It was not everyday that he got such a request from a ten year old child.

"These are not regular herbs, boy," said the trader. "These are mihika herbs. People smoke them and have fun."

"But isn't it a crime to sell such herbs?" asked Soumil.

"A man has to do whatever it takes to survive," replied the trader. "Every criminal doesn't get punished, and every honest man doesn't get rewarded."

"I agree," said Soumil.

Soumil again asked the trader to teach him how to sell the herb. The trader refused initially, but when Soumil persisted, he gave him a few tips. He then told Soumil about Mihika Nagari, where he could get the finest supply of the herb.

By the time he was sixteen, Soumil had become a mihika trader of some standing. He bought the herb from Mihika Nagari and sold it to people all over Jivavarta for a good profit.

One day, while in Mihika Nagari, Soumil heard that a very important man from Trishala was around. This man, called Viraj, was a frequent visitor, and had a liking for the herb. Seeing a potential customer, Soumil approached him.

"My lord," said Soumil, "I hear that you come here all the way from Trishala in search of good mihika herb."

Viraj was amused to see the young boy, dressed as an adult, and trying to talk to him as an adult.

"Yes, I do," said Viraj. "How does it concern you, boy?"

"I know how important you are, and how important your time is for you," said Soumil. "Instead of you coming here, I can deliver the finest mihika herb to you in Trishala."

Viraj was interested in the proposition. He did waste a lot of time coming to Mihika Nagari. But he was skeptical of the young boy pulling a fast one on him.

"You can," said Viraj. "But you are not going to get any advance karshikas from me."

"That's fine, my lord," said Soumil. "You can pay me later, that too only if you are satisfied."

Viraj looked at Soumil. He was very impressed.

"How old are you, boy?" asked Viraj.

"I am sixteen, my lord," replied Soumil.

"You have the age of sixteen, but the shrewdness of a sixty year old," smiled Viraj.

Soumil smiled back. He liked the compliment.

"My name is Viraj," said Viraj. "When you are in Trishala, tell my name to the palace guards. They will bring you to me."

Soumil took a bow, and moved on, scouting for more customers.

After ten days, true to his word, Soumil met Viraj in Trishala with the finest mihika herb he had ever seen.

Viraj was so glad that he didn't mind paying double the street price.

"Aren't you too young for this trade, boy?" asked Viraj. "Don't your parents say anything?"

"My father is dead," said Soumil, "and my mother doesn't have to know."

"Where do you live?" asked Viraj.

"In the Khara marshlands," said Soumil.

Viraj was curious. He could see that Soumil earned enough to afford a decent living in a city.

"I didn't realize that you were a tribal," said Viraj.

"No, I am not," said Soumil. "We are hiding from the Rongchas."

Soumil was glad that this had come up. He knew that Trishala was not friendly with the Rongchas, and all along he had been thinking about how to broach the topic with Viraj.

"Why?" asked Viraj, getting even more curious now.

Soumil narrated the story that he had heard from his mother since childhood.

"What is your mother's name?" asked Viraj. There was a sense of urgency in his voice.

Soumil realized that he might have misjudged Viraj.

"Don't give us to the Rongchas, my lord," he pleaded. "They will kill us."

"What is your mother's name, boy?" repeated Viraj.

"My mother name is . . . " Soumil couldn't complete his sentence.

"Griha?" asked Viraj.

Soumil couldn't believe his ears. How could Viraj know?

Seeing the shock on Soumil's face, Viraj knew that he was right.

He embraced Soumil. After years of separation, Viraj had found his family.

"I am your uncle," his voice choked. "Take me to my sister, nephew."

Soumil couldn't hold his tears either. After years of wondering about the uncle who had saved his life, here he was, right before him.

They rushed to the Khara settlement to meet Griha.

"Daras, you are alive!" Griha smiled. It had been a long sixteen years.

"Yes, sister," smiled Viraj. "Now I go by the name Viraj."

Soumil proudly told his mother that Viraj was now a trusted adviser of the king of Trishala.

"Come and stay with me," said Viraj. "You don't have to hide from the Rongchas anymore."

Griha declined. With some other widows in Khara, she had decided to become an Ajabuhi monk, and serve the people who had supported her all these years.

When back in Trishala, Viraj introduced Soumil to the king. Tasvak was impressed with what Viraj told him about Soumil, and gave him a position in the palace staff.

Soumil was grateful for the trust the king had shown on him. He was thankful for this opportunity, and vowed to serve his king well.

52

COMPASSION OF THE KING

King Tasvak regularly visited the Dhataki settlements on the border of Yashantika and Trishala. In time, Soumil started accompanying Tasvak on these visits, and could see Tasvak's compassion for Dhatakis, which seemed strange given Viraj's contempt for them.

In one of these visits, Soumil found the courage to ask Tasvak.

"My king," he said. "I can understand you being compassionate towards tribals. But how can your treat these beastly Dhataki people with so much compassion? Why are you taking so much effort for their betterment?"

Tasvak knew where Soumil's hatred for Dhatakis came from. Viraj had never hid his dislike for the Dhatakis, and had also tried to convince Tasvak to stay away from them.

"Don't call them beastly," said Tasvak. "That makes it easy to justify treating them badly. For me, there is no difference between the nobles, the commoners, the tribals, and the Dhatakis. All of them are hardworking people who are trying to progress through all the bad treatment they get, through all the problems they have."

Soumil agreed. He could see that Tasvak was right, and Viraj's contempt was unfounded.

"What you are doing for the victims of the raids is praiseworthy, my king," said Soumil. "I was once at the receiving end of a Yashantika raid."

He had Tasvak's attention.

"Were you?" asked Tasvak.

"Yes, my king," said Soumil. "A few years back, we were staying in a village in the Vidari settlement. It was a peaceful, prosperous village of honest and hardworking tribals."

He glanced at the king, who was listening intently.

"Suddenly, one day, Yashantika soldiers attacked," he continued. "They rushed into the village, and burned everything in their path. As the villagers panicked and ran, they chased them. The younger villagers were taken as cetas, and the elderly were killed."

"In just a few moments, it was all over," sighed Soumil. "The village was destroyed completely. Each house looked like a pyre. We were among the handful who survived."

Tasvak nodded. He could now understand the hardships the tribals were facing. He realized that rebuilding the settlements was not enough. These raids had to be stopped.

Later that day, Soumil narrated his conversation with the king to Viraj.

"I see that you are in awe of King Tasvak," said Viraj, sensing Soumil's devotion.

"Yes, I am," confessed Soumil. "He is what I had always dreamed of becoming."

"Never keep anyone on pedestal," said Viraj. "If someone you have kept on a pedestal falls, it hurts badly."

Soumil smiled. He had kept Viraj on a pedestal since he was a child.

53

THE FALLOUT

"On this auspicious day, let us together pray for the prosperity of our lands," said Tasvak, as he welcomed King Jaskar Dharman and Chief Snuhi to Trishala.

Tasvak had decided to use the Varti celebrations to get Jaskar Dharman together with Snuhi, and convince him to sign a peace treaty.

"I agree," said Jaskar Dharman.

Although he was upset about Chief Snuhi being treated as an equal to him, nobody could have guessed that from his calm appearance.

"Let us forget what happened in the past," he added, looking at Snuhi. "At least for today."

"I want to forget what happened, but my heart doesn't allow me to," said Snuhi, bitterly. "Every time my heart aches for my only child, I think of you."

Jaskar Dharman nodded.

"You shouldn't have kidnapped my son and forced him to marry your daughter," he said. "You kept my son in captivity, and were punished for that."

"Kidnapping grooms for marriage is our tradition, not keeping them captive," countered Snuhi. "Your son stayed with us with his own will, because he hated going back to you."

Jaskar Dharman smiled, and looked away. He didn't like the tribal savage talking to him with such disrespect.

After the celebrations, Tasvak tried to propose a peace treaty between Yashantika and Vidari, but Jaskar Dharman brushed away the idea.

"There is peace everywhere," he said. "We don't need a peace treaty."

"There is peace in Vanpore, perhaps," said Tasvak. "But Yashantika soldiers are killing hundreds of people everyday."

"My soldiers attack these savages because they refuse to accept Yashantika's authority," said Jaskar Dharman.

"Surely you can convince these tribes peacefully," said Tasvak. "So many tribes willingly accept Trishala's authority."

Jaskar Dharman remembered the day, not too long back, when Tasvak had desperately approached him for help. And now, he had the audacity to advise him on how to run his kingdom.

"Is that your pride speaking, King Tasvak?" asked Jaskar Dharman. "Should I be worried?"

He had sensed a threat in the way Tasvak was talking to him. It was clear that Tasvak was no longer afraid of the might of Yashantika.

"If you continue these raids, then yes, you should be worried," answered Tasvak. "But not because of me. When they get tired of all this unnecessary violence, your own people will revolt."

"My citizens don't have a problem with violence," said Jaskar Dharman. "It is normal for them."

"When the people of a state think that violence is normal, then it is a failed state," said Tasvak. "The tribals listen to me because I treat them as one of us – because that's what they are."

"This is not you who is speaking, King Tasvak," said Jaskar Dharman. "This is that monk Trivit, and his teachings. I don't need any advice on what I should do with my kingdom."

When the meeting ended, it was clear that the relations between Trishala and Yashantika were no longer cordial.

54

THE PRINCE AND THE PRIEST

Prince Yashthi had often wondered how he will respond if he ever gets captured by the enemy. He had pictured himself standing fearlessly before his captors, his head held high, holding them spellbound with his royal aura.

But now, when he was actually captured by Trishala soldiers, there was no royal aura. Instead, there was a dejected man, walking barefoot through the mud, with his hands tied behind his back.

As he stopped, wondering about his fate, he felt the pull of the chain tied around his neck.

"Don't stop until we tell you to," the soldier walking beside him shouted. "Keep walking."

Yashthi resumed walking, the cold metal chain hurting him on every step.

A short while later, another soldier shouted "Stop and bow to us, mighty prince."

Prince Yashthi stopped, and bowed. He hated doing this, but he had no choice. He heard the soldiers laughing at him.

He cursed himself, for he alone was responsible for this situation.

Just a day earlier, he was leading the raid on an Ajabuhi monastery near the border in Trishala. The raid had gone well, and they had destroyed the monastery. He could then have gone straight to Vanpore. Instead, on his way back, he decided to look around for a suitable location for the Tapasi temple his father was planning to build.

He wanted to keep his plans a secret, so that he could surprise his father. He sent his bodyguards back to Vanpore with the troops. He was confident that no Trishala soldier will dare to enter so deep into Yashantika.

But he was wrong. A small troop of Trishala soldiers patrolling the border had heard of the raid on the monastery, and had crossed over to Yashantika in search of the perpetrators.

He was alone in the forest when they captured him.

"Who are you?" asked a soldier.

"I am Prince Yashthi of Yashantika," said Yashthi.

They laughed at his face. Yashthi was dressed in simple robes, just like his father, and looked like a commoner.

"Look, what we have here," chuckled one soldier. "A prince of Yashantika roaming alone in the forest."

"Should we kill him?" ventured another soldier.

"What if he really is a prince of Yashantika, as he says?" said another, a saner voice, who seemed to be their leader. "Let us take him to the general, and let him decide."

So, they had tied him up in chains, and were now taking him to their general, who was on the other side of the river.

By the time they reached the river, it was dusk. There was a small boat tied to the shore, swaying in the water, and there was no sign of a boatman.

"All seven of us can't cross the river in this small boat," said the leader.

He pointed to the strongest soldier in the group.

"You go to the general," he said. "Ask him what to do, and then come back."

"This is a difficult task," the soldier responded. "After reaching there, I don't think I will be able to row back."

"Don't come back, then," said the leader. "Stay there and give a message."

"How can I give a message from the other side of the river?" asked the soldier. "I can't shout that loud."

The leader pondered for a moment. Then, he pointed to a small temple on the opposite bank. There were three lamps on the side facing them.

"Go to the temple, and light the lamps," said the leader. "If the message is to let him go, light one lamp. If the message is to hold him, light two, and if the message is to kill him, light all the three lamps."

Everybody agreed that this was a great idea.

Prince Yashthi was confident that no general in his right mind will think of harming a Yashantika prince. They may use him as a bait for negotiation, but harm him – never.

The soldier hopped into the boat, and started rowing. Soon, the boat vanished into the darkness.

One hour went by, and then two. The soldiers were getting restless waiting for the signal.

Then they noticed that one lamp in the temple was lit.

"Only one lamp is lit," said one soldier. "We should let him go."

Prince Yashthi gave out a sigh of relief.

"Wait, don't decide in hurry," said another soldier. "I see that a second lamp is lit."

"We should hold him, then," said the first soldier.

Yashthi was disappointed. He wondered how long this ordeal will last. Not for too long, he hoped – he desperately wanted to be back in his palace. He needed a warm bath.

Meanwhile, on the other side of the river, the soldier responsible for sending the message was having a heated argument with a priest in the temple.

"Why did you light only two lamps?" the priest was saying. "You need to light all the three lamps."

"It is a signal, priest," the soldier was trying to convince. "I am just following the general's orders."

"Lighting only two lamps is a bad omen," declared the priest. He was adamant.

"Please understand," the soldier tried again. "If I light

all the three lamps, a man will lose his life."

The priest wasn't listening. He was not comfortable with the soldier getting in the way of his chores, and did not have the patience for all this talk about signals and some man losing his life.

"If you don't want to light the lamp, I will do it myself," said the priest, and lighted the third lamp.

"Please don't do this," pleaded the soldier. "You don't understand. Stop!"

He rushed forward, but the priest stood between him and the lamps.

"Stay away," said the priest. "To touch the lamp, you will have to get past me."

The soldier didn't want to attack the priest. He stood there, wondering what to do next.

The soldiers on the other bank were still looking at the lamps.

"I see that all the three lamps are lit," said the first soldier.

"Yes," said the second soldier. "All the three lamps are lit."

"I see them, too," said the leader.

The soldiers looked at Yashthi. There was a long silence.

"This means that the order is to kill," said the leader, as he took out his sword.

Prince Yashthi panicked as he realized the gravity of the situation.

"No, stop," he pleaded. "Please listen, there is some

misunderstanding. Your king will never ..."

Before Yashthi could finish his sentence, the sword struck.

The prince of Yashantika was dead.

55

THE UNFORTUNATE
MISTAKE

Jaskar Dharman read the message from King Tasvak again and again.

"A man who calls himself Prince Yashthi has been captured by Trishala soldiers. They are holding him on suspicion of destroying an Ajabuhi monastery. As an act of goodwill, I have asked them to hand him over to Yashantika soldiers this time. In return, I expect Yashantika's attacks on the Ajabuhi monasteries to stop."

Jaskar Dharman had initially thought the message was in jest. How did they manage to capture Yashthi? Why did his soldiers not inform him?

He summoned the commander of the troop who had accompanied Yashthi on the raid.

"What happened at the Ajabuhi monastery?" asked Jaskar Dharman.

"We were successful," replied the commander. "We killed all the monks and destroyed the monastery."

"Where is Prince Yashthi?" asked Jaskar Dharman.

"On our way back, Prince Yashthi said that he needed to explore some place inside the forest," said the commander. "He insisted on going there alone."

"He insisted, and you let him go?" Jaskar Dharman was furious.

"Prince Yashthi said taking soldiers and weapons will destroy the peace of that place," replied the commander. "He even sent his bodyguards with us."

Jaskar Dharman was upset. He couldn't believe Yashthi had been so careless.

To make sure, he walked to Yashthi's chamber. Yashthi was not there. His cetas informed the king that he had not returned since he left for the raid.

Then he sent his best soldiers to search for Yashthi around the area where he had separated from the troops. The soldiers came back empty handed.

Now sure that Yashthi had indeed been captured by Trishala, Jaskar Dharman waited impatiently for his return.

After three days, a messenger from Trishala arrived with a request for an urgent meeting between King Tasvak and King Jaskar Dharman. It was agreed that they will meet near the border.

The kings met at the appointed place. Jaskar Dharman had no time for pleasantries. He anxiously looked around for his son.

"It was a misunderstanding," said Tasvak, as he broke the news. "My general had instructed the soldiers to hold the prince. But due to an unfortunate miscommunication, Prince Yashthi lost his life. There is no excuse for what happened. I am very sorry for your loss."

Tasvak kept explaining in detail how Prince Yashthi's death was a misunderstanding, an unfortunate mistake, and without any motive. He was visibly pained.

Jaskar Dharman stood there, listening to Tasvak's every word. He wanted to ask Tasvak, "What kind of soldiers do you have, who don't listen to their general?" He wanted to strangle Tasvak with his bare hands. But he didn't do any of that. He just stood there expressionless. He wondered what he was going to tell his wife.

"It is not your fault," he said, finally. "We can't control everything, do not trouble yourself."

Jaskar Dharman was saying all the right things, but his eyes were saying "You are going to pay for this."

Tasvak nodded, acknowledging Jaskar Dharman's gesture. But he knew that this was not the end.

56

THE PLAN

"Why have you called a meeting to negotiate with Trishala?" asked Jivak. "I thought you wanted revenge for brother Yashthi's death."

After his son's death, Jaskar Dharman had waited for a few weeks. Then, he had sent a message to Tasvak, asking Trishala to double its tribute to Yashantika.

As Jaskar Dharman had expected, Tasvak had politely declined. So, he had now called a meeting between Yashantika, Rongcha, Adrika, and Trishala to renegotiate the tributes paid by Trishala to the other three kingdoms.

"I have called this meeting because I want a war against Trishala," answered Jaskar Dharman.

"I don't understand," said Jivak. "Aren't the negotiations about maintaining peace with Trishala?"

"Yes, they are," said Jaskar Dharman. "But I know that

these negotiations will be unsuccessful."

"How can you be sure?" asked Jivak.

"I know that Tasvak will not agree to an increase in the tributes," said Jaskar Dharman. "But King Dhanveer of the Rongchas is a greedy, arrogant fool. He will not back off the chance to get more money."

"I want war," he added. "But I want King Dhanveer to start it."

Everything so far had been happening as Jaskar Dharman had planned. He was looking forward to the meeting, and had ordered his troops to prepare for the imminent war.

57

THE GOD AND HIS KINGS

Rongchas believed that in the beginning of time, god had descended to Igati. He liked Igati so much that he decided to make it his home.

He then asked for human sacrifice. On a day that was now celebrated as the Prahuti festival, two men and a young boy offered themselves, and were sacrificed on the altar. Pleased, the god decided to reward the three. He resurrected the first man, and made him the king of Adrika. He then resurrected the second man, and made him the king of Yashantika. Finally, he resurrected the young boy, and made him the king of Trishala. The god himself became the king of Rongcha.

So, when the invitation to the meeting arrived, King Dhanveer was furious.

"How dare Jaskar Dharman invite me to a negotiation!" shouted King Dhanveer. "I don't negotiate. I am the god of Jivavarta, and I decide what happens here."

"So you are not going, father?" asked Princess Guduchi.

"I will go," said Dhanveer. "I don't like that fanatic Jaskar Dharman, but I support his demand of doubling the tribute."

"Trishala is flourishing, and we need a part of that wealth," he added. "If that mlechcha Tasvak thinks that he can dictate the terms, I will destroy him and his tribal army, and annex Trishala."

Guduchi was not comfortable with her father's stand. He had refused to attack Trishala when the Rongcha soldiers were evicted from Trishala, and decimated by Tasvak and Yashantika's army. He had let Trishala prosper all these years. Now, Trishala had a strong army, the best of weapons, and the support of ruthless tribals. Rongchas had no chance of winning against them.

But she knew that her father was too arrogant to reason with, and left quietly to prepare for his departure for the meeting.

58

PRINCE VIVANT

"People who live in the past should not decide the course of the future," said Prince Vivant. "Why should a handful of highborns decide who does what, who eats what, and who learns what? That too, based on a few scriptures written in another era."

Vivant always had his way with words, thought Queen Abhadevi.

"What if we give the people the freedom to mingle, to intermarry?" asked Vivant. "There will be no highborns and lowborns in Adrika, everybody will be equal."

"You are right, my son," said Abhadevi. "But, as rulers, we have to behave responsibly. We are not at liberty to enforce such sweeping social reforms. We don't have power over people's minds. If we force people to follow our beliefs, they will revolt. They will think that we are tyrants trying to control their lives."

Vivant knew that his mother was right, but all this did not make any sense to him.

"I see unjust social conditions everywhere, and I want to change them," he said. "But if we try to change these conditions, we lose the throne. Even with so much power, we are powerless."

Vivant was visibly frustrated.

"What is the use of this throne, if I can't do what I want?" he continued. "I don't care about being the ruler, and I don't care about behaving responsibly. I want to do what is best for the people. If to do so, I need to have power over people's minds, then that is the power I want instead."

"Vivant, enough!" said Abhadevi, sternly. "If somebody hears that you don't want to become the king, there will be serious consequences. Your uncle Briham has been eyeing the throne for a long time."

It pained her to chastise Vivant, but these were difficult times. Rivals as well as family members were conspiring for the throne of Adrika. They hated Abhadevi's courage, and they hated taking orders from a woman.

After her husband's untimely death, she had became a queen regent to Vivant. She had expected Vivant to assume his responsibility as a king now, but his progressive thoughts shocked her.

Vivant looked at his mother, and quietly walked out of the room.

He had been thinking about leaving it all behind. He

knew that his mother was a great ruler, better than he could ever be. And, in a few years, his younger brother Revant would be old enough to help her.

"Today is the day," said Vivant to himself, and left the palace.

There was no looking back. He spent the next several years in relentless pursuit of the real power, the power over people's minds. He roamed all over Jivavarta, met people, and did whatever was needed to gain that power.

Now, fifteen years later, he was the most influential monk in Jivavarta. He was no longer Prince Vivant – he was now Guru Trivit.

59

THE MONK AND THE QUEEN

Queen Abhadevi had prevented Ajabuhi from spreading in Adrika as she found the faith too progressive for her liking. She had also never showed any interest in meeting Guru Trivit. But when her advisers told her that Guru Trivit was the only person who could influence King Tasvak, she had reluctantly asked for a meeting.

She arrived at the Ajabuhi monastery in Vakshi, and was quietly led into a room. It was evening, and Guru Trivit was in meditation.

"Please wait here, Queen Abhadevi," said the monk who had led her in. "Guru Trivit will join you in a moment."

After a short wait, Trivit entered the room. It was almost sunset, and Abhadevi couldn't see his face clearly.

"I am Queen Abhadevi of Adrika," she said. "I am here to ask for help."

There was something very familiar about the guru's presence.

"What help do you need, mother?" asked Guru Trivit.

Mother? She knew that voice. Startled, she looked at Trivit's face.

"Vivant?" she gasped in disbelief. It was her son.

"Yes, mother," replied Trivit, and lowered his head in respect.

Abhadevi couldn't hold her tears. After so many years, she cried.

Trivit let her cry. As she calmed down, Trivit again asked her the purpose of her visit.

Abhadevi understood. She was here as the queen of Adrika, to meet an adviser of the king of Trishala. There was much at stake here, the mother will have to wait.

"I want you to prevent a war between the three kingdoms and Trishala," she said.

"Prevent a war?" asked Trivit. "But don't the three kingdoms already have a treaty in place with Trishala?"

"Yes, we have a treaty," explained Abhadevi. "But recently, King Jaskar Dharman had requested for doubling the tribute, which King Tasvak declined. King Jaskar Dharman has now called a meeting of all the kingdoms to negotiate with King Tasvak. King Tasvak has refused to attend the meeting, saying that he has no reason to negotiate."

Trivit was listening attentively. He had not been aware of these developments.

"If King Tasvak does not attend the meeting, King Jaskar Dharman and King Dhanveer will push for an attack on Trishala," Abhadevi continued. "I am here to request your help in convincing King Tasvak to attend the meeting. Adrika doesn't want a war."

"I don't know whether King Tasvak will listen to me," said Trivit.

"Do not lie to me, Vivant," said Abhadevi. "I have heard about how much King Tasvak depends on Guru Trivit. Everybody knows who holds the actual power in Trishala."

"That's an overstatement," smiled Trivit. "But maybe I can help if you promise to encourage the people of Adrika to adopt Ajabuhi."

Abhadevi had not seen this coming.

"Are you bargaining with your own mother?" asked Abhadevi.

"I am not bargaining," said Trivit. "I am only doing what is good for the people."

"I will try," Abhadevi relented. "But the people of Adrika might not be willing to accept a new faith."

"That's enough for me," smiled Tasvak. "Now, enough of these problems, mother. Tell me about Sonira. How is Revant? What all has happened in the last fifteen years?"

"Fifteen years is a very long time, my son," Abhadevi sighed. "There is so much to tell you."

60

THE REVEAL

"Welcome, monk," said Tasvak. "How was your stay in Vakshi?"

Soon after his meeting with Queen Abhadevi, Trivit had requested an urgent meeting with Tasvak.

"It was very productive, my king," replied Trivit. "I met Queen Abhadevi of Adrika."

Tasvak now realized what this meeting was about. He was not happy about Abhadevi using Trivit to influence him into increasing the tribute.

"What did she want from you?" asked Tasvak, bitterly. "Is she joining Ajabuhi?"

"She wanted me to convince you to join the negotiations," answered Trivit.

"I declined to attend the meeting because I refuse to increase the tributes to these kingdoms," explained Tasvak. "If I do so, it will be a severe drain on Trishala's resources."

He looked at Trivit with a resolve in his eyes.

"We can't avoid the unavoidable," Tasvak added. "If it comes to that, Trishala is ready for the war."

Trivit shook his head.

"You misunderstand," said Trivit. "Queen Abhadevi wants peace. She fears that if you don't agree to attend the meeting, Jaskar Dharman and Dhanveer will force a war."

Tasvak was surprised. He had not realized that Abhadevi was on his side.

"In fact," added Trivit, "Adrika is ready to accept a decreased tribute."

This gesture sounded too good to be true.

"What does Adrika gain from this?" Tasvak asked.

"A strong and independent Trishala is in the interest of Adrika," explained Trivit. "Trishala is the barrier that saves Adrika from the aggression of Yashantika and Rongcha."

This made sense to Tasvak. He pondered for a moment.

"But can we trust Queen Abhadevi?" asked Tasvak. "Maybe this is a trap to lure me to the meeting."

Trivit smiled at the thought.

"I assure you, my king," he said, "Queen Abhadevi is not capable of such treacherous behavior."

His confidence surprised Tasvak.

"How can you be so sure, monk?" he asked.

"I know her very well," replied Trivit. "She is my mother."

For a moment, Tasvak did not know what to say. He recalled the afternoon in Vakshi when Trivit had mentioned that he was from Sonira, and how fondly he had talked about the city, and the palace.

"So you are the crown prince of Adrika who had left many years ago?" asked Tasvak.

"Yes, I was that prince," smiled Trivit. "Now, I am an Ajabuhi monk, who likes to work for peace and equality in Jivavarta."

"I respect you for that," said Tasvak. "You can tell Queen Abhadevi that I will attend the meeting."

"Thank you, my king," said Trivit. "I am grateful."

"Time after time, you surprise me with your secrets," said Tasvak. "First, you revealed that Zirosthi is my grandfather. Now, you reveal that Queen Abhadevi is your mother."

"That I do," said Trivit, with a mischievous smile.

As Trivit left, Tasvak wondered what other secrets he might be hiding.

61

MOTHER'S WISH

Adrika welcomed its long lost prince with open arms. There were festivities all over Adrika in honor of Guru Trivit. But nobody was happier than Revant.

"I am so happy that you are back, brother," smiled Revant. "I have always wondered about you."

"Did I live up to your expectations?" asked Trivit.

"You are much better, and beyond my expectations," said Revant. "But you have changed so much. I still remember the short-tempered boy who used to say whatever came to his mind. Mother was always afraid of you insulting the nobles with your sharp comments."

"That boy is still there," smiled Trivit. "But I smother him every morning after I get up."

Revant wondered why his brother's calm persona scared him more than his earlier aggressive one.

Queen Abhadevi kept her promise. She encouraged the adoption of Ajabuhi among the people. In a matter of days, many new Ajabuhi monasteries were opened across Adrika, and Trivit and Revant personally oversaw the enrollment of new followers. Working with his brother, Trivit was glad that he was back in Adrika.

"You should take the throne," Trivit told Revant.

"Did mother talk you into this?" said Revant. "But why? Even though I am not the king, I do help mother in her duties."

"The people think that you enjoy the perks of a king, but don't want the responsibility," said Trivit. "You need to prove them wrong, and earn their respect."

"But the throne is yours, brother," said Revant.

"Now it is yours," said Trivit. "You rule Jivavarta with the throne. I will rule with the faith."

Revant laughed. Surely, Trivit was trifling with him.

"To rule Jivavarta, we need to start wars against the other kingdoms," said Revant.

"No," said Trivit. "We only need to start wars amongst the other kingdoms."

Revant realized that Trivit was serious. He pondered for a moment.

"What about King Tasvak?" asked Revant.

"What about him?" asked Trivit, looking at Revant.

"Nothing," replied Revant. But Trivit knew what he meant.

"There is nothing to worry about," assured Trivit, "as long as you listen to my advice."

Prince Revant gave in to his brother's wishes, and agreed to become the king.

Abhadevi was overjoyed on hearing the decision. She had saved the throne for her sons for a long time, and was relieved to pass on the responsibility.

After the coronation, Abhadevi told her sons that she had no other aspirations in her life, and informed them of her wish to take the "vow of fasting". She wanted to fast until death.

"This is nothing but suicide," said Trivit. "Join Ajabuhi, mother. Become a monk."

"I lived my whole life following others' wishes," said Abhadevi. "Let me follow my own wish in my death."

Trivit and Revant had no choice but to respect her last wish.

62

THE NEGOTIATIONS

Vakshi had always prided itself as the "city of peace". Today, it was hosting four kings for a meeting to renegotiate the peace treaty with Trishala.

The first to arrive was the new king of Adrika, King Revant. He was accompanied by his brother, Guru Trivit. Then came King Jaskar Dharman of Yashantika, followed by King Tasvak of Trishala, and finally King Dhanveer of Rongcha.

Jaskar Dharman was surprised to see Guru Trivit, but didn't say anything. Dhanveer was more vocal about his displeasure.

"What is this monk doing here?" he asked, pointing at Trivit.

"He is our guru, and he is here to advise us," replied Tasvak.

"Do you see my guru with me?" shouted Dhanveer. "Keep faith out of diplomacy and politics. Even this fanatic Jaskar Dharman knows that much."

Trivit smiled, and calmly walked out.

Jaskar Dharman started the meeting by thanking everybody for accepting his invitation.

"We have two issues before us," he said. "First, I propose doubling of the tribute paid by Trishala to each of our kingdoms. As we all know, Trishala is far more prosperous now than when we agreed on the current amount. The prosperity has increased over the years, but not the tribute."

"Second," he added. "We need to agree on how to deal with the tribal settlements. Trishala has been, for some time now, opposing Yashantika's raids on the tribal settlements. Ajabuhi monks, with King Tasvak's support, have been helping the tribals resettle after the raids, and also converting them to the Ajabuhi faith. This needs to stop."

He then nodded at Tasvak, and asked him to respond.

All eyes were on Tasvak now. He took a deep breath, and looked at Jaskar Dharman.

"You are right, King Jaskar Dharman," said Tasvak. "Trishala is more prosperous now. This means that Trishala no longer needs any external help. So, there is no reason anymore for Trishala to continue paying the tributes."

King Dhanveer looked at Tasvak with outrage.

"But, as a goodwill measure," Tasvak added, "and in appreciation of your help during Trishala's dark days, Trishala is willing to pay a reduced amount. I propose reducing the tributes to half the current amounts."

"As for the second issue," Tasvak continued, "how Trishala treats its tribals is not up for discussion, as it is our internal matter. I again request Yashantika to stop its raids on the helpless tribals immediately."

King Dhanveer was running out of patience.

"Enough of all this nonsense," he shouted. "I am the god of Jivavarta. Only my decision counts, and I order Trishala to double the tributes."

He then looked at Tasvak.

"And what do you mean by your internal matter?" he scoffed. "I refuse to accept Trishala as separate kingdom. Trishala is mine, and I decide what happens there. You support those tribals because you are one of them. You killed my son-in-law so that you could marry that mlechcha girl."

Tasvak was trying hard to control his anger. He did not want to succumb to the provocation and upset the meeting.

"The tribals deserve the treatment they get," Dhanveer continued. "I do not support anyone helping them, and I do not recognize the Ajabuhi faith."

Tasvak ignored Dhanveer, and asked King Revant to speak.

"I accept Trishala's proposal for decreasing the tributes," said Revant. "Also, I declare Adrika's support for the work King Tasvak and Guru Trivit are doing for the tribals, including spreading the Ajabuhi faith among them."

King Dhanveer was furious.

"How dare you?" he shouted at Revant.

King Jaskar Dharman smiled, and looked at Tasvak.

"I admire your noble intention to treat all humans equally," he said. "But God Sarvabhu has created us differently. You must embrace your role as the king, and keep these mlechchas in their place at all times. It is for their own good. They may complain at times, and plead for sympathy, but this is what Sarvabhu intended for you, and for them. If you do otherwise, you will face Sarvabhu's wrath."

He glanced around the room.

"I accept Trishala's proposal for decreasing the tributes," Jaskar Dharman continued. "But I strongly disagree on breaking the established social norms."

King Dhanveer was livid on hearing that even Jaskar Dharman was now supporting the decrease in the tributes.

"Double the tribute, or be ready to face the consequences," he threatened Tasvak. "I am going to annex Trishala, and throw you out."

Tasvak was raging in anger, but didn't respond. He recalled what Guru Sarvadni had told him once, "Confronting your enemy in anger feeds your ego, but diminishes your chance of success."

His face red with anger, Dhanveer stood up and stormed out of the room.

After Dhanveer was gone, King Jaskar Dharman continued.

"I have every reason to hate you," Jaskar Dharman said, looking at Tasvak. "But to keep peace in Jivavarta, I agree not to attack the tribals in Trishala. In return, you need to ensure that the Ajabuhi faith does not cross into my kingdom. Do you agree?"

"I agree," replied Tasvak. He didn't want to anger Jaskar Dharman while under Dhanveer's threat.

It was settled, then. The significant reduction of the tributes, and the stopping of raids on the tribals by Yashantika were both major wins for Trishala.

But this pact didn't go well with Trivit.

"You shouldn't have promised Jaskar Dharman that Ajabuhi will not be imposed in Yashantika," said Trivit.

Tasvak was surprised at this criticism.

"I thought Ajabuhi is all about not imposing your beliefs on others," said Tasvak. "If Ajabuhi does that, then there is no difference between Tapasi and Ajabuhi."

"That's true," said Trivit. "But sometimes, you have to impose your beliefs on others. Not everybody is capable of deciding what is good for them."

Tasvak couldn't take it anymore.

"Guru Trivit," he said, "I am grateful for your support in making Trishala a great kingdom, and I will seek your counsel whenever needed. But the affairs of my kingdom are best left to me."

Although the words were uttered politely, the displeasure in Tasvak's voice was apparent.

"How dare you talk to Guru Trivit like this?" said Revant, in a surge of anger.

Before Tasvak could reply, Trivit intervened.

"King Tasvak is right, brother," he said. "He did what is best for his kingdom."

Tasvak nodded, and Trivit smiled. Everything seemed to be back to normal.

63

THE WRATH OF THE GODS

Dhanveer left Vakshi feeling humiliated. As soon as he was back in Igati, he called his generals, and told them to conduct raids on Trishala's villages.

Princess Guduchi tried to warn her father.

"Trishala is no more a vulnerable trading port," she said. "It is now a prosperous kingdom with a strong king and a powerful army. They can now defend against our attacks. They may even retaliate."

Guduchi, who had taken over as the commander of the Rongcha army after her husband's death, knew that the Rongcha army was in shambles. The kingdom was grappling with lack of funds, and had not been able to pay its soldiers well. Also, the humiliating defeat a few years back at Trishala had left the soldiers demoralized. They were certainly not ready for a war.

But Dhanveer refused to listen.

"How can they retaliate?" he asked. "Do you think Tasvak is foolish enough to attack Igati? Nobody has ever won against Rongchas. We are the gods."

"But father," said Guduchi, "we need to be careful."

"If you are so afraid, go ahead and jump from the Heaven's cliff," thundered Dhanveer. Heaven's cliff was the Rongcha royals' private gateway to heaven. It was believed that whenever a Rongcha royal jumps from the Heaven's cliff, he goes straight to heaven.

Rongcha soldiers started conducting raids on Trishala's villages. But, as Guduchi had feared, they were no match for the Trishala soldiers. They were invariably chased away, and often suffered heavy casualties. Soon, any further raids became untenable.

Dhanveer felt even more humiliated now. He was now bent on teaching Tasvak a lesson.

"We have to find some other way to weaken Trishala," he told Guduchi.

He sat in his council room, stared out of the window, and thought hard. The prestige of the mighty Rongchas was at stake.

64

THE EDICTS AND THE FEAST

King Tasvak's return from Vakshi was met with cheer from the people.

The significant reduction in the tributes meant greater prosperity, and lower taxes. The people now regarded Tasvak as a compassionate ruler who was working for their betterment.

Also, the promise by Yashantika not to attack Trishala's tribal settlements brought relief to the tribals. They no longer needed to be under constant fear of attack. As a result, many more tribes accepted Trishala's authority over them.

Building on his increasing popularity, Tasvak decided to take the next step. To seal his support for social reforms, and to formally promote the teachings of Ajabuhi among the people, he decided to issue edicts under his name.

The edicts were:

- King Tasvak, the follower of Ajabuhi, says that all humans are equal.

- King Tasvak, the follower of Ajabuhi, says that all humans will be judged by their deeds and not by their birth.

- King Tasvak, the follower of Ajabuhi, says that no human is the property of any other.

- King Tasvak, the follower of Ajabuhi, says that widow immolation is an inhuman act of cowardice.

- King Tasvak, the follower of Ajabuhi, says that a king must serve the people and not rule by divine right.

- King Tasvak, the follower of Ajabuhi, says that people must forget the past and adapt to the new.

Tasvak invited Guru Trivit to release the edicts. Much to his relief, Trivit readily agreed. Tasvak was now satisfied that things were indeed normal between them.

To mark the event, Queen Avani organized a feast. It was a grand celebration, attended by nobles, tribal chiefs, Ajabuhi monks, and select delegates from Trishala's lower town. Singers and dancers entertained the guests while they enjoyed their food – a lavish spread, prepared under Avani's personal supervision.

"Why are you not eating anything?" Tasvak asked Avani. "You look exhausted."

"I am fasting for your good fortune, and the future of Trishala," she smiled, and asked her maid to get the special tea that the cook had prepared for her.

"I will drink this," she said, as the maid arrived with the bowl. "It is enough for me."

Hungry and thirsty after a hard day's work, she started drinking the tea, and seemed to relish it.

Sitting by Tasvak's side, Avani cheerfully talked about how Trishala is now so different, and far more prosperous, than what she had seen as a child. She talked about their son, Abhik, and wondered if he would also grow up to be as brave and compassionate as his father.

After her tea was over, Avani got up to talk to the guests. She moved swiftly, going from table to table, making sure that everyone was having a good time.

Tasvak couldn't help looking at her. Avani noticed Tasvak, and responded with an adorable smile. Tasvak had barely looked away, when he heard a thud.

Avani had collapsed. There were cries and confusion for a moment, and then there was complete silence. All eyes turned towards Tasvak.

Tasvak rushed towards Avani. She was lying still on the ground, blood dripping from her mouth. He fell down to his knees, and desperately tried to revive her as he lifted her in his arms. He was unable to make sense of what had happened.

He closed Avani's lifeless eyes, and kept still for a moment, looking at her. Then he cleaned off the blood from her face with his robe, and lovingly kissed her forehead. Overcome with grief, he kept tightening his grip on Avani's body. He tried to remain calm, but as he realized the extent of his loss, he couldn't control himself. His sobs turned into screams that ripped through the stunned silence of those around him.

This was murder, a cowardly move to weaken him. But he was not going to take the cowardly path, he was going to annihilate those who killed Avani, while confronting them face to face.

No words could describe his sorrow and his hate.

65

THE MARCH TO IGATI

The cook had confessed that it was the Rongchas who had paid him to poison the tea. For Tasvak, this was a declaration of war.

Minister Kathik had tried to dissuade Tasvak from attacking Rongcha, saying that nobody had ever been able to capture Igati, but had to relent against Tasvak's resolve.

Tasvak had summoned his war council, and put forth his plan for the attack. The council had agreed, and Trishala's troops were now on their way to Igati.

They were now in Rongcha territory, camped in the foothills of the Sahiya mountains. The villages around were deserted – the word of the impending attack had spread fast, and the people had retreated to Igati.

"We start climbing tomorrow," said Viraj. "Will you join the soldiers for drinks tonight?"

"No, you go ahead," replied Tasvak.

"You should start mingling more," said Viraj. "It has been more than three months now."

"Ninety seven days," said Tasvak.

"What?" asked Viraj.

"It has been ninety seven days since Avani left me," said Tasvak.

"Are you really counting the days?" asked Viraj. He was concerned.

"When you lose your soulmate, you don't just count the days, you count every single moment," replied Tasvak. "When you love some one, they become a part of you, and when they go away, you don't know who you are without them."

"We are getting worried about you," said Viraj.

Tasvak looked at Viraj.

"Don't worry," he said. "I am perfectly fit to lead the troops, if that is what you are concerned about."

Viraj smiled, and tried to change the subject.

"Do they ever leave you?" he asked, looking at the Lokharo bodyguards standing at the entrance of the tent.

"Yes, they do," replied Tasvak. "When the other group of Lokharo bodyguards takes their place."

"They don't look scary to me," said Viraj, "I can take them down if they fight fair."

"They never fight fair, they fight to win," said Tasvak. "They are not nobles like you, who fight by their code of honor."

"I am not a noble," said Viraj. "I am just a glorified assassin. I don't have a position in your court."

"I didn't give you a court position because you deserve much more than that," said Tasvak. "You are my closest friend."

Viraj wanted to make clear that he wasn't happy to be just the closest friend. But he didn't get a chance, as Soumil entered the tent.

"Everything is ready, my king," Soumil told Tasvak. "The carts are painted as you instructed."

"Very good, Soumil," said Tasvak. "Did you inform the troop leaders?"

"Yes, my king," replied Soumil, "The troop leaders will gather here in the morning."

"Why did you have to appoint those tribals as troop leaders?" asked Viraj.

Viraj was not comfortable fighting beside the tribals. He had never considered them as his equals, despite his Ajabuhi faith teaching him otherwise.

"They are leading troops of their own tribesmen," explained Tasvak. "They understand their men's behavior, customs and language better than anybody else."

"But they are savages," said Viraj.

Tasvak was getting annoyed.

"They are not savages," he said. "They are just like us. We need to look beyond our differences to achieve a common goal."

Viraj nodded. He did not agree, but knew that this was not the time to argue.

"We have to start early tomorrow," said Tasvak. "So,

let's eat. Soumil, would you like to join us?"

"Thank you, my king," said Soumil. "But I am not hungry."

As Soumil left, Viraj let out a sigh.

"He is so composed," said Viraj. "Sometimes I wonder if Soumil is my nephew, or I am his."

"I agree," said Tasvak. "Soumil is mature for his age. He has taken so much responsibility. Once the war is over, I am going to promote him."

"If you give him a position in the court," Viraj said, "I am going to kill myself."

Tasvak wasn't listening. He was deep in his thoughts, figuring the plan for the next day.

66

THE SURPRISE

It was morning, and Tasvak stood in front of his troops.

"My warriors, no one in the history of Jivavarta has ever done what we are going to do. We are going to take over Igati."

The soldiers cheered. They all had supported and accepted Tasvak as their king with all their heart. They had every reason to, as their life had improved tremendously since Tasvak had become the king. They believed they were on the side of good, and they were fighting for what is right.

"We are fighting for what is ours. Why should we pay tributes to other kingdoms? I tried to reason with King Dhanveer, but he didn't listen. He kept raiding and burning Trishala's villages. He even had Queen Avani murdered."

Tasvak looked at the soldiers. They were listening to his every word.

"Now, it is time to fight back," he thundered. "It is time to fight for our honor!"

Battle cries charged up the atmosphere. "For honor! For Trishala!"

Tasvak waited for the battle cries to cease. Then he continued.

"Rongchas expect us to climb the gold route. But along that route, they will be watching our every move. They will be waiting at Igati to trap and kill us. But we are not going to fall into their trap."

Tasvak paused for a moment.

"We are going to climb the Anantavat."

There was silence. Anantavat – literally, the unending climb – was another route to reach Igati. It was a notoriously difficult climb, and nobody in living memory had been known to scale it.

"You might have heard stories about Anantavat. It is not an easy climb. The weather is bad. Rongchas have poisoned the streams, so there is no drinkable water. They have planted poisonous plants along the way, so there is no food except what you carry. The path is laden with bodies of those who attempted the climb, but failed."

There was a slight disquiet among the soldiers.

"The Lokharos will lead us on the climb. But this is not going to be an easy road. Whoever wants to go back, is free to go back. It won't be held against you."

To Tasvak's surprise, nobody left. Instead, there were

battle cries from all the directions.

"For honor! For King Tasvak! For Trishala!"

After the soldiers had dispersed, Viraj approached Tasvak. The plan had taken him by surprise.

"When was this decision taken?" he asked.

"A week back," replied Tasvak.

"I was not informed about this plan," said Viraj. "Don't you trust me?"

"I trust you," said Tasvak. "I trust you more than anybody else. But I also know that you would have tried to talk me out of the decision."

"For sure, I would have," said Viraj. "This is a crazy plan. Horrible death is certain for all of us."

He pondered for a moment, then shook his head.

"Your life is too important, you must go back to Trishala," said Viraj. "Let me go ahead, I will lead the troops up the Anantavat."

"I know that you are ready to sacrifice your life for me," said Tasvak. "And I know that this is a dangerous mission. But I want to lead it myself."

Viraj sighed, and accepted Tasvak's wish. It was too late to change the decision now. He wished he had known about this earlier.

"Who else knew?" asked Viraj.

"Only Soumil and the Lokharos," replied Tasvak.

"Soumil, why didn't you tell anything?" Viraj asked Soumil, who was standing beside Tasvak.

"Because I told him not to," said Tasvak.

Viraj nodded. He had one last concern.

"If the Rongchas don't see us on the gold route, won't they figure that we are climbing Anantavat?" asked Viraj.

"We are sending these carts as a decoy along the gold route," replied Soumil, pointing towards the painted carts.

Viraj looked at carts carefully. They were painted to give an illusion that they were marching troops of soldiers.

"Let us move," ordered Tasvak.

67

THE UNENDING CLIMB

As Tasvak's troops reached the Kahalava pass, Zirosthi was waiting for them.

"I know that you will return victorious," said Zirosthi, embracing his grandson.

The Lokharos welcomed the soldiers with the traditional Lokharo wine.

"May you drink so much that you lose your fear, but not so much that you lose your mind," cheered Zirosthi, as he offered the wine to Tasvak.

Soon, the troops were on their way, with a group of Lokharos guiding them. By evening the next day, they had crossed the roaring Hirika river using an old hanging bridge, and had started the stiff climb to Igati. This was the Anantavat.

As they walked on, the landscape changed. Soon,

there was snow all around them. Some soldiers, who had never seen snow before in their life, were awestruck and scared. The sky was clear, but the melting snow had lowered the temperature, and made the path slippery. Further up, the path became narrow and treacherous, and they had to progress slowly and carefully.

After a while, it started becoming dark, and the temperature fell further. The soldiers were exhausted and hungry, and the sparse air at the high altitude made them sick. They took rest at nightfall – but because there was no shelter, they had to sleep in the open, lying exposed as frost set in.

In the morning, the aftermath of the harsh cold in the night was visible. A few soldiers had frozen to death. Several others had fallen ill, and were not in a state to continue the climb.

As he carried on with the remaining soldiers, Tasvak wondered whether he had made a mistake. What right did he have to risk so many lives? He asked the soldiers. They replied that they wanted freedom from the eternal liability of paying for the tributes, and they were ready to die for it. They remembered how the Rongchas had put Trishala under siege, how they had treated the people, and wanted them to pay for their excesses. They assured Tasvak that they were with him, no matter what.

"For honor! For Trishala!" the soldiers cried in the biting cold. They had to endure just two more days of hell before they reached Igati.

68

THE HUNTER AND THE HUNTED

"Father, you are looking divine in your armor," said Guduchi.

The compliment made King Dhanveer look up with a smile. He had decided to wear the armor everyday since he learned that Trishala's troops were on their way. The Rongchas had always attacked others, and this was a rare occasion that someone was attacking Igati. Dhanveer was excited.

"I am wearing an armor after a long time," said Dhanveer. "It feels great."

"We will win," Guduchi assured him.

"Of course, we will," said Dhanveer. He did not need the assurance – Igati had never been captured in the history of Jivavarta.

In fact, Dhanveer had already pictured Tasvak being brought before him in chains after the battle, and had given some thought on how he would make Tasvak pay for the humiliation at Vakshi.

Guduchi stared out of the window of the council room. She was looking at the marching Trishala troops, a tiny speck far below, down the gold route.

"How long before they reach?" Princess Guduchi asked her general.

"They are moving slowly, my lady," said the general. "At this rate, it will take them a couple of days."

"Hold the fire," said Guduchi. "Wait until they are in the range."

Three days passed. Trishala's troops were still not in the range.

King Dhanveer was losing his patience.

"What are you waiting for?" thundered Dhanveer, in his shining armor. "Send the troops down, chase them, and destroy them."

"But father," protested Guduchi, "if move our troops, who is going to protect Igati?"

"Protect Igati from what?" asked Dhanveer. "Trishala's soldiers are not going to fall from the sky. If you are scared of fighting, stay here. I will lead the troops."

"I am not scared," said Guduchi. "But we should not underestimate Tasvak. I can go down and attack Trishala's troops tomorrow, but I believe that we will be losing the advantage of a superior strategic position."

Dhanveer was in no mood to argue.

"Do as I say!" he shouted. "Don't forget that I am your father, and your king. My word is final."

"As you wish, father," Guduchi relented.

Next morning, Guduchi and a large number of Rongcha soldiers marched down the gold route, towards the approaching Trishala troops. They went on for half a day. But the further they went, Trishala's troops appeared to be even farther away. They kept chasing, and were led far down, into the valley.

"My lady, this does not seem right," said her general.

"The orders are to chase and destroy them," Guduchi said. "Move faster."

After some time, they finally caught up. But all they found were painted carts. The actual soldiers were nowhere to be seen, and whoever was towing the carts had quietly fled on their arrival.

"This is a decoy," the general panicked. "There are no soldiers."

Guduchi realized what had happened. Her fears had come true.

"This was trap to lure us from Igati," shouted Guduchi. "We need to get back. Fast!"

"Get back where, my lady?" asked the general. "Look above."

Guduchi looked above. Igati was burning, and a thick cloud of smoke had covered the Rongcha palace.

She and her soldiers desperately rushed to Igati. But by now, the Trishala soldiers were in control of the

Rongcha firearms. As soon as they were in range, the Rongcha soldiers were greeted with fire arrows and barrels of hot oil. The battle did not last long. It ended with the Rongcha soldiers meeting the same fate that they had in mind for the Trishala troops.

For the first time in the history of Jivavarta, Igati had fallen.

69

THE BLINDSIDE

Tasvak and his soldiers had scaled Anantavat in three days. After reaching Igati, they had hid themselves on the outskirts and kept a watch on the gold route. Tasvak predicted that Dhanveer will soon lose his patience, and dispatch his troops to attack what he thought was Trishala's army. He was right, and as soon as the troops left, they swooped into the city. There was barely any resistance as they took over the palace.

Dhanveer had not seen this coming. He tried to put a brave front, but realized that it was too late. He preferred to die a king than being captured, so he escaped to the Heaven's cliff, the royal gateway to heaven. Closing his eyes, he called out to his ancestors, and jumped. As his body went down thousands of feet before hitting the ground, King Dhanveer Rongcha ascended to the heavens.

When the news of Dhanveer's suicide reached Tasvak, he was disappointed.

"I wanted him to confess to Avani's murder," said Tasvak.

"You can ask his daughter," said Viraj. "We have captured her alive."

Princess Guduchi had not resisted her capture. She did not care what happened to her now, her only concern was the safety of her young son. She was fearless as she was brought before Tasvak.

"Why did your father poison my wife?" Tasvak asked. "What had she done to him?"

"Where are my father and my son?" asked Guduchi.

"Your father committed suicide at the Heaven's cliff, and your son is safe in my custody," said Tasvak. "Now answer my question, why did your father poison my wife?"

Guduchi was relieved that her father had not been taken a prisoner. She knew that he would not have taken that humiliation lightly. She felt a rage against Tasvak, but controlled her anger for the sake of her son.

"My father could not have poisoned anybody," she responded. "Rongcha royals can only kill people in combat using a weapon. For us, poisoning anybody is an unforgivable sin."

"She is telling the truth, my king," said Soumil. "I asked some of the captured soldiers. They say that if a Rongcha royal poisons somebody, he will be damned for eternity, and will never reach salvation."

Tasvak was stunned. He looked at Viraj.

"Why didn't you catch the cook's lie?" he asked Viraj. "As a Rongcha, you should have known."

Viraj looked embarrassed.

"I am not a religious person," he replied. "And I have been away from Rongcha for a long time. I did not know this."

Tasvak was disappointed, but he was glad that Dhanveer's tyranny had ended. He recalled what his soldiers had told him in Anantavat, on what this victory meant for them. The people of Trishala had finally taken their revenge on the Rongchas.

Viraj told Tasvak that the soldiers were looking forward to raid Igati, to complete their revenge. Tasvak refused, and warned against any such act.

"But these are the subjects of the evil king Dhanveer," insisted Viraj.

"Don't confuse the actions of a ruler as the nature of his people," Tasvak replied sternly.

Tasvak freed Guduchi, and appointed her as the queen of the Rongchas, giving her the right to rule the Rongcha kingdom in the name of the king of Trishala. He held her son as a hostage, and sent him to the Kahalava pass to be raised among the Lokharos.

"Your son is safe until you remain loyal to Trishala," he assured Guduchi. "Also, a few Ajabuhi monasteries will be opened in Rongcha to help improve the lives of the people, but you and the people will have the freedom to follow your faith."

Guduchi had no choice but to comply, as her son was in Tasvak's captivity. But she promised herself that she will fight again one day, and bring her son back.

As he was bringing the matters at Igati to a close, Tasvak received a message. Guru Trivit was in Igati, and wanted to meet him urgently.

70

THE USURPER

Tasvak had been waiting in the council room of the Rongcha Palace, wondering what could have prompted Trivit to rush all the way to Igati to meet him.

"I have bad news for you," said Trivit. "There has been a coup in Trishala. Kathik has taken control of the kingdom."

Tasvak let the news sink in for a moment, and sighed. He was concerned about his son, who he had left in Kathik's care.

"Prince Abhik is alive," said Trivit, rightly guessing Tasvak's thoughts.

"I always knew that Kathik was a slimy worm," said Viraj. "I will start preparing for an attack on Trishala."

"You can't attack Trishala," said Trivit. "Prince Abhik is Kathik's hostage. He is unharmed at the moment, but a direct attack will put his life in danger."

"I underestimated Kathik," said Tasvak. "I agree that a direct attack is not an option for now. We need to think of an alternative."

"You need to be careful," said Trivit. "Jaskar Dharman seems to be behind all this."

Tasvak nodded. He had guessed as much.

"What does Jaskar Dharman have to do with this?" asked Viraj.

"Don't you see?" said Tasvak. "If Dhanveer didn't poison Avani, then who has gained from it?"

"Kathik," said Viraj. "If it were not for Queen Avani's death, you would not have attacked Igati, and Kathik would not have gained control of Trishala."

"Kathik is a coward," said Tasvak. "He is not capable of taking such a big step on his own."

"A number of Yashantika soldiers can be seen in the Trishala palace since you left," said Trivit. "This suggests Jaskar Dharman's support to Kathik."

Viraj agreed, this indeed suggested Jaskar Dharman's involvement. In his days at Vanpore, Viraj had worked for Jaskar Dharman, and knew that he was capable of such a conspiracy.

"But what could be his reason to conspire against you?" he asked. "After all, he helped you capture Trishala from the Rongchas."

"Jaskar Dharman has a reason," answered Tasvak. "He is extracting his revenge from me for ordering the killing of his son."

"But you never ordered the killing," said Viraj. "It was a misunderstanding."

"Jaskar Dharman never believed that," said Trivit.

Tasvak was trying hard to control his rage.

"Jaskar Dharman has to pay for what he did," he said. "He always told me that he hates me, but what did he have against Avani?"

"Hater you can find in a moment," said Viraj, "but it takes an eternity to find a true well-wisher."

"Because there are no true well-wishers," said Trivit. "Every person has some motive behind his every action."

"You don't have a motive," said Tasvak, looking at Trivit. "Still, you are helping me."

"I have a motive," said Trivit. "I want peace and prosperity for the people of this land."

As Trivit left, Tasvak looked out of the window. He had been blindsided by Kathik. The way out now was to blindside Kathik in return.

71

THE WOUNDED AND THE HEALERS

"We all are wounded, and we all are healers. As the time changes, the role changes," said the carving on Chief Snuhi's throne.

How apt, Tasvak thought, as he waited for Snuhi.

Chief Snuhi had enough reasons to be grateful to King Tasvak. Tasvak had taken care of, and returned his grandson. Also, since the treaty with Trishala, the Vidari tribals were getting good price for their produce. Moreover, due to Tasvak's efforts, Yashantika's raids had stopped and the victims of earlier raids had been resettled.

So, when Tasvak came to meet him, Snuhi was pleased, but surprised.

"I am very glad that you have come to visit me," said

Chief Snuhi, courteously.

"I have come to visit you under very strange circumstances," said Tasvak. "I am here personally because I need a favor from you, under the promise of secrecy."

Snuhi nodded.

"You must have heard that Kathik has taken over Trishala," said Tasvak.

"Yes, I have," said Snuhi.

"I have my troops at my disposal," said Tasvak. "But I cannot attack Trishala as my son is in Kathik's custody."

"I see," said Snuhi, cautiously. "But how can a lowly chief like me help you?"

"I need you to visit Trishala and meet Kathik," said Tasvak. "You will go under the pretext of offering luxury gifts to the new king, and renewing the treaty with Trishala. My men will accompany you and take control of the palace."

Snuhi shook his head.

"Why should I do that?" he said. "What's in it for me? For my tribe?"

Tasvak had not expected that he will need to negotiate, after all that he had done for Snuhi and his tribe. But he took it in his stride.

"Kathik is Jaskar Dharman's puppet," said Tasvak. "If he remains the king of Trishala, the trade treaty between you and Trishala will be repealed, and Jaskar Dharman will resume the raids on Vidari."

Snuhi nodded, but did not agree yet. He was aware of the consequences, but had realized that he was indispensable in Tasvak's plan. He was waiting for Tasvak to raise the ante. It did not take long.

"If you do this, I will provide your tribe with weapons," said Tasvak. "Vidaris are courageous people, but are vulnerable to attacks. I will provide your people with weapons, and also train them to defend themselves."

Snuhi looked interested now.

"Why do I need to go personally?" he asked. "I can send a few of my men with the gifts."

"It must be you," said Tasvak. "Kathik will not be able to refuse a meeting with the chief of the Vidaris."

"What happens if I die in Trishala?" said Snuhi. "You will get your son back anyhow. But my grandson will lose his grandfather, and my wife her husband."

"You need not worry," said Tasvak. "I will be sending my trusted men as your bodyguards. My general, Soumil, will accompany you as well. Once they get an entry into the palace, you can leave. They won't attack until you are back to safety."

Snuhi thought for a moment, and agreed.

Tasvak gathered his best men. Under the charge of Soumil, they accompanied Chief Snuhi to Trishala with the most luxurious gifts Kathik would have ever seen.

72

In Vain

Before leaving for Rongcha, Tasvak had appointed Minister Kathik as the caretaker ruler. Kathik had dutifully accepted, and assured Tasvak that he will serve loyally to the best of his capabilities.

Kathik had served as a minister for many years, starting way back under King Vighasa, then under King Nahusha, and now under King Tasvak. But this was the first time that he had the full charge of the kingdom. It did not take long for him to realize how much he liked his new status. He liked the attention that he was getting. He liked the way people bowed to him. He liked being the ruler.

He also knew that Tasvak was not coming back. Nobody in the history of Jivavarta had ever come back alive after attacking Igati. On his part, he had tried his best to stop Tasvak, but Tasvak had not listened.

A few days after Tasvak left, Kathik had received a message from Jaskar Dharman, extending support to him as the king in the eventuality of Tasvak's death. For Kathik, this was as good as being recognized as the rightful ruler – it was just a matter of time now, he thought. Kathik felt blessed, and gratefully welcomed the Yashantika soldiers Jaskar Dharman had sent to control any opposition to his taking the throne.

But Tasvak did not die. He miraculously defeated the Rongchas and captured Igati. Everybody at Trishala celebrated this unexpected and unprecedented victory, except Kathik. To Kathik, this victory meant leaving the charms of being the ruler, and getting back to his old job.

Kathik did not want his old job. He did not want to get back to being an unappreciated minister. He deserved the throne, and he was going to keep it.

He declared himself as the king of Trishala.

He did not have to worry about Tasvak. As long as he had Tasvak's son in his custody, Tasvak would not dare to retaliate. The nobles didn't object after Kathik convinced them of their brighter future. The soldiers in Trishala's standing army found themselves outnumbered by the Yashantika soldiers, and decided to wait and watch. But the people of Trishala couldn't bear to see their beloved king being deposed. They revolted against Kathik.

Kathik contacted Jaskar Dharman for help, but he refused to support the coup. Not willing to give up, Kathik offered hefty payments to the Yashantika soldiers, and persuaded them to help him contain the revolt.

This worked initially. But now, after weeks of chaos, things were getting difficult. Trade was at standstill, so there was no income. The payments to the Yashantika soldiers were fast depleting the treasury. The soldiers in Trishala's standing army, who were not getting paid as a result, were close to joining the revolt.

Kathik had neither the charisma, nor the shrewdness of Tasvak. He was getting overwhelmed, and desperately needed money.

So, when Chief Snuhi of Vidari requested an audience with Kathik to offer tribute to the new king, and renew the trade treaty he had with King Tasvak, Kathik accepted readily.

Chief Snuhi arrived with a group of men carrying an array of valuable gifts as the tribute. Kathik welcomed Snuhi and his men into the palace with open arms, and humbly accepted the tribute offered. They signed the treaty, and celebrated the occasion.

Snuhi left soon after the meeting, citing an urgent matter that needed his attention back in Vidari. He left behind a few of his men, who lingered on unnoticed in the palace.

Kathik was too preoccupied to care. He was delighted at this windfall. The tribute was enough to buy a month or two of peace, he estimated. By then, he should be able to figure something out. Relieved, he slept peacefully that evening – only to be woken up around midnight by footsteps outside his door.

Kathik called his guards, but there was no answer. He

cautiously came out of his chamber, and looked around. His guards were dead. Realizing that something was very wrong, he rushed to Prince Abhik's chamber, where he found Abhik surrounded by Soumil, Viraj, and a few men who, he recalled, had accompanied Chief Snuhi earlier that day.

"Do you really believe that a handful of you can take over Trishala?" said Kathik, putting on a brave face. "Leave now, or I will call my soldiers."

"Why will the soldiers listen to you?" asked Soumil.

"They will listen to the ruler of Trishala," said Kathik, trying his best to intimidate the intruders. "I am the ruler of Trishala."

"No," said Soumil. "They will listen to the true ruler of Trishala, who he is here to claim his throne."

Viraj got hold of Kathik by his neck, and dragged him to the throne room.

The throne room was dark. But in the moonlight, Kathik could see the face of the man who was sitting on the throne. He knew this face.

Kathik fell down on his knees. He knew that any resistance was futile.

"Forgive me, my king," Kathik pleaded. "Jaskar Dharman put all this into my mind. I was merely his puppet."

He looked powerless and fragile, almost pitiable.

"I know that you were a puppet," said Tasvak. "But you willingly played the part."

Kathik was in tears. He knew that his game was over.

"Did you plan Queen Avani's poisoning too?" asked

Soumil.

Kathik gasped.

"Speak," said Tasvak, sternly.

"I knew about the plan," said Kathik. "But I swear on my ancestors, my king, I had nothing to do with it."

"What about Jaskar Dharman?" asked Soumil. "Was it his plan?"

"I don't know," replied Kathik. "I don't now what part Jaskar Dharman played."

"Are you lying to me?" thundered Tasvak.

Kathik saw the gleam of a sword in the moonlight. He was too scared to speak anymore. He knew that any moment now, Tasvak was going to chop his head off. He ran out, screaming desperately for help.

Viraj ran after Kathik. Suddenly, there was a loud crash. As Tasvak and Soumil rushed out, they saw Kathik's body lying lifeless, face down in the garden below. He had tripped over the railing in the dark, and fallen headlong to his death.

"Kathik died the way he lived," said Viraj. "In vain."

"I wanted him to tell the truth before he died," said Tasvak.

"He told it all by jumping to his death," said Viraj. "You are right, it was Jaskar Dharman."

73

THE GROUND UNDER THE FEET

After his return, Tasvak took some time bringing Trishala back to normal. That done, he left the day to day activities of the kingdom to Viraj, and started preparing for an attack on Yashantika.

Yashantika was a far superior force than Rongcha. The army needed better weapons and, to compensate for the lives lost at Anantavat, it needed to recruit soldiers and train them. There was much to be done, and there was not enough time.

Amidst all this, a stormy visit from Zirosthi came as a surprise.

"You are preparing for war against other kingdoms," said Zirosthi. "But what about the battles happening in your own kingdom?"

The question confused Tasvak.

"There is no battle happening in my kingdom," he said. "I would have known."

"Do you really know?" asked Zirosthi. "Do you know about the burning of Tapasi temples in Rongcha? Do you know that entire families are being burnt alive if they refuse to follow Ajabuhi?"

Tasvak found this hard to believe. Ajabuhi monks were sent to Rongcha to help people, not burn Tapasi temples, or force conversions.

"Ajabuhi is a faith of peace, not of violence," said Tasvak. "I will ask Guru Trivit to check if any such incident has happened, and punish those responsible."

"You are blinded by your trust in that monk Trivit," said Zirosthi. "Do whatever you want, but keep Lokharos out of this. They are never going to follow this faith. Do not try to force them."

"Nobody will force Lokharos to follow Ajabuhi," assured Tasvak. "I will see to that."

"Wake up, king," said Zirosthi, as he left. "Don't be like your mother. Her blind trust on your father got her killed. I hope the same doesn't happen to you."

Tasvak immediately discussed Zirosthi's concerns with Viraj and Trivit. Neither of them was aware of any untoward incidents such as those mentioned by Zirosthi.

Trivit assured Tasvak that everything was normal, and Zirosthi had been misled by false rumors. Surely, these rumors were being spread by Jaskar Dharman to defame

Ajabuhi.

These rumors upset Tasvak, and increased his hatred for Jaskar Dharman. He needed to end this menace once and for all.

74

THE SIEGE OF VANPORE

Yashantika had never faced such a powerful enemy.

Trishala's army was no longer the army of traders that Yashantika's soldiers had fought years back. It was now much superior in its weapons, discipline, and strategy.

Yashantika's army had tried to stop Trishala's troops at the border. But Tasvak had an answer for every move that Yashantika made. Even Yashantika's tactic of sending Dhataki soldiers to scare the enemy had not worked – the Dhatakis were no match for the fearsome Lokharo soldiers Tasvak had set on them.

As Trishala's troops progressed, Yashantika's army was forced to retreat to Vanpore. Trishala's troops had then laid siege on the city, waiting for surrender.

It had been almost two months now, but there was no word from Jaskar Dharman.

"How long will they be able to hold?" asked Soumil.

"Long enough," replied Viraj. "Vanpore has grains in store which will last for almost a year."

"Jaskar Dharman will not wait for one year," said Tasvak. "He is waiting for the rains."

"Why?" asked Soumil. "What happens during the rains?"

"Once the rains start, river Girika will be flooded," explained Tasvak. "It will cut off our food supply, and we will be vulnerable. That is the time Jaskar Dharman will attack."

"What are we waiting for, then?" said Viraj. "Let us shoot fire arrows into the city and burn it down."

"Currently, the people of Vanpore are strongly behind King Jaskar Dharman," said Tasvak. "If we burn the city, it will be an all-out war. There will be fatalities on both sides. We need to find a way to reduce the people's support for Jaskar Dharman."

He looked at Viraj.

"Can you get in touch with Khoram?" asked Tasvak.

"I can try," said Viraj. "But he is a worthless worm."

"Doesn't matter," said Tasvak. "Bring him to me."

Viraj took a few men and went across to the Dhataki settlement. In a few hours, he was back with Khoram.

Khoram had not changed much in the years since Tasvak had seen him last.

"Are the Dhatakis still cleaning Vanpore's sewage?" asked Tasvak.

"Of course," said Khoram, proudly. "Without the

Dhatakis, Vanpore will turn into a rotting hell in a week."

Tasvak nodded.

"Khoram, would you like to join our army?" he asked directly.

Khoram took a step back. He looked surprised at the offer.

"I am not a fighter," he replied. "Also, I am a loyal servant of King Jaskar Dharman."

"Let's not play games with each other," said Tasvak. "That you agreed to meet me means that your loyalty is for sale. What is the price?"

Khoram gave a broad smile.

"Five thousand gold karshikas," he said.

"Three thousand gold karshikas," countered Tasvak, "and you will join Ajabuhi."

"Four thousand gold karshikas," said Khoram, his smile broader now.

Tasvak stared at him for a moment.

"I told you not to play games," he said. "I can kill you this moment, and force your people to follow my orders. Take whatever I am giving you. You have no choice."

Khoram stepped back in fear. His smile had disappeared.

"I ... I ... I agree, my king," he relented.

With the Dhatakis on his side, Tasvak ordered them not to clean the garbage and sewage from Vanpore. After a few days, he had them stealthily block the drainage outlets feeding into the trench outside Vanpore's wall.

All he had to do now was wait.

75

THE ROTTING HELL

The Dhatakis had abandoned Vanpore.

The garbage in Vanpore started piling up and, with the sewage outlets blocked, the drains started overflowing. As Khoram had predicted, the city became a stinking, rotting hell.

The people of Vanpore were not used to handling filth. Even as the sewage started getting on the roads, they were clueless and too disgusted to unclog the drains. When the garbage started rotting, they tried to burn it, but gave up as they could not bear the smoke and the stench.

Within a month, people started falling sick. Rats were visible everywhere, and the possibility of plague made people very nervous. They started speaking about truce with Trishala.

King Jaskar Dharman had planned to deal with

scarcity of food, but not with a flood of garbage. He had never imagined that the city was so vulnerable and dependent on the lowly Dhatakis. Faced with protests, he tried to convince the people to have patience for just one more month, until the start of rainy season. But to the people, it was clear that rains would bring more misery to them than to the army outside. They wanted a solution immediately.

Jaskar Dharman's plan had failed. There was no alternative now, but to get back to the battlefield. He called the generals to persuade them to attack the Trishala army. In face of the humiliating defeats earlier, he knew that convincing them was not going to be easy.

"Brave generals of Yashantika," started Jaskar Dharman, "Vanpore is under attack. Our existence is under attack. Our faith is under attack."

He glanced around the room. All he could see were weary faces. He was disappointed, but continued.

"If we wait any longer, there is a chance that we will die of plague. Instead, why not attack now? We have won many glorious battles in the past, we will win this too. Let us fight for Yashantika."

The generals knew that certain death awaits them in the battle with Trishala. For them, it was a lost cause, and no speech could be powerful enough to push them to their death.

"Let us fight with glory for Tapasi and Sarvabhu," Jaskar Dharman appealed.

The generals could not hide their resentment anymore. They blamed Jaskar Dharman for the sorry state of affairs.

"Where is the glory in getting slaughtered by the Trishala army?" asked one general.

"Your incompetence has brought this on us," shouted another. "You allowed Trishala to become this powerful."

"Let us make peace with Trishala," said the first general. "Let us surrender. Tasvak is not a warmonger. He will understand. He will spare our lives."

"Let us surrender," shouted the generals.

Jaskar Dharman did not want to face the humiliation of a surrender. But by the time the meeting ended, Jaskar Dharman had realized that if the situation continues, his own people will depose and kill him.

He needed to think of something else.

76

THE TRUCE

"Ready to talk truce, I know that you are man of peace."

Tasvak looked at the message from Jaskar Dharman. His Dhataki gambit had worked. Vanpore had been brought down to its knees.

His response was immediate.

"The people of Vanpore should not die because of your wrongdoings. You alone should suffer the consequences. I challenge you to a duel to avenge the murder of Queen Avani."

When Jaskar Dharman received the message, he went silent for a moment.

"Will you accept the challenge?" asked Jivak.

"Why should you accept the challenge?" asked Queen Dishadevi. "You did not poison Queen Avani. Did you?"

"No, I did not," said Jaskar Dharman. "But I knew of

the plan."

"Then send a reply saying that you did not poison Queen Avani," advised his wife.

"Do you think my message is going to convince him?" asked Jaskar Dharman. "After all, I did help Kathik. Tasvak has already made up his mind."

"Then what you are going to do?" asked Dishadevi.

"Accept the challenge, and defeat him in the duel," said Jivak. "Then tell him that you didn't kill Avani."

"I can't defeat Tasvak in a fight," said Jaskar Dharman.

"Why not?" asked Jivak. "You are one of the greatest fighters I know."

"I have won ceremonial fights, not actual fights," said Jaskar Dharman. "I don't even remember when was the last time I entered a battleground. Tasvak has the training of a warrior, and the mind of an assassin."

"So, what will you do?" asked Dishadevi. She was getting worried.

"I have no other option but to accept the challenge," said Jaskar Dharman. "If I don't, the people will revolt and join him against me."

Dishadevi was stunned. She knew that this was suicide. In desperation, she went to plead with Tasvak.

"How can you bring this on us?" she asked. "We helped you when you needed our help. We forgave you, even though your soldiers killed our son. My husband knew of the plan to kill your wife, but he did not kill her."

"I am sorry for your loss, Queen Dishadevi," replied Tasvak. "But I didn't kill Prince Yashthi. I did not know that he was being killed. Had I known, he would be alive today."

Queen Dishadevi nodded.

"But your husband knew about the plan to murder Avani," Tasvak continued. "He could have stopped it, but he didn't. That makes him responsible. If King Jaskar Dharman can convince me otherwise, I will cancel the duel, and go back to Trishala."

Dishadevi looked at Tasvak, silently pleading for forgiveness. But Tasvak had made up his mind. He had been wronged by her husband, and he wanted revenge. Dejected, she went back to Vanpore.

The date of the duel was fixed, and the preparations began. But everyone knew that the duel was a mere formality – Trishala had won the war.

A day before the duel, Tasvak was pleased to welcome Trivit. He had invited Trivit to oversee the conversion of Khoram and other Dhatakis to Ajabuhi, and set up a monastery to help uplift their lives. Trivit was accompanied by his brother, King Revant.

The presence of Revant surprised Tasvak. He had neither been invited, nor had a reason to be present there. He wondered what the real purpose could be.

77

THE DUEL

The duel was a solemn affair.

Jaskar Dharman arrived in his royal armor, without any fanfare, accompanied by only a handful of guards. He knew what the outcome of the duel was going to be, and the despair showed on his face.

He fought bravely, but could not hold his ground against the younger and stronger Tasvak. It wasn't long before he was too exhausted to fight. All he wanted now was an end to the humiliation.

"Kill me, and spare my people," said Jaskar Dharman, panting heavily. "Please allow my family to cremate my body."

Tasvak nodded.

"I promise," he said. "But I need an answer. Who was behind the plan to kill Avani?"

Jaskar Dharman looked at Tasvak.

"You will not believe me," he replied. "It was Trivit."

Tasvak was indeed too angry to believe Jaskar Dharman. He was sure that it was another of his lies. Jaskar Dharman had always hated Trivit.

"It was Trivit who hatched the plan," Jaskar Dharman said, with great effort. "After you left Vakshi, Trivit and Revant met me in confidence and shared the plan with me. Trivit had decided to eliminate you, and have Revant take over Trishala."

"What does this have to do with Avani's poisoning?" asked Tasvak. "If they wanted to eliminate me, they could have poisoned me."

Jaskar Dharman shook his head.

"Poisoning you would have led to a revolt in Trishala," he said. "You needed to die in a battle."

He took a deep sigh, and resumed the narrative.

"Trivit convinced the cook, who was his loyal follower, to poison Avani and blame Dhanveer. He knew that you will attack Rongcha to take your revenge. You were expected to die in combat there, while Revant took over Trishala."

Tasvak was listening. He realized that this was a confession of a dying man, who had no reason to lie now.

"Trivit asked me to remain neutral," Jaskar Dharman continued. "He promised me half of Trishala's wealth in return. I agreed because I was angry with you after my son's death."

Jaskar Dharman looked at Tasvak for a moment, then

looked away as he resumed.

"But I did not trust Trivit," he said. "So, I blocked his plan by supporting Kathik to take over as the king after you died. But when I learned that you were alive, and have won the war against the Rongchas, I withdrew my support to Kathik."

"Why did you do that?" asked Tasvak.

Jaskar Dharman smiled.

"I have always hated you," he said. "But you are the son I never had."

Tasvak was taken aback. But he knew that Jaskar Dharman was not innocent. He was telling the truth now only because it did not matter to him anymore. He was as much a party to Avani's murder as any of the others. He could have saved Avani if he wanted, but he did not.

Tasvak felt his rage building up as he thought of Avani, how she had been killed for no fault of hers. He had failed to save her from these monsters. He wanted revenge for her. Tasvak felt the world around him dissolve into a haze as he raised his sword, and slashed Jaskar Dharman's throat.

He then stood there as the guards picked up Jaskar Dharman's body and carried it away. He stood there for a while, staring at the ground, oblivious of his soldiers cheering at a distance. Suddenly, he felt very tired. Still in a haze, he drifted back to his tent.

Alone in his tent, he lied down and thought of Avani. He thought about what all Jaskar Dharman had said. He thought of the face of the dying old man.

He realized that the pursuit of revenge against Jaskar Dharman had been more satisfying than the actual act of killing him. Nothing had changed. He was still unhappy, and still yearned for Avani.

Slowly, he let sleep take over him.

78

THE WAR VILLAINS

Tasvak had no idea how long he had slept. When he woke up, it was unusually quiet outside.

He thought about what Jaskar Dharman had told him, and decided to confront Trivit.

"Ask Guru Trivit to meet me," he told his guard.

"Guru Trivit has left for Vakshi," said the guard. "He was here to inform you, but you were sleeping."

"Where is Viraj?" asked Tasvak.

"He and King Revant are raiding Vanpore with the help of Dhatakis," replied the guard.

"Raiding Vanpore?" Tasvak asked in disbelief. "Why?"

He had promised Jaskar Dharman that the people of Vanpore will not be harmed.

"They are following Guru Trivit's orders," said the guard. "Guru Trivit said that now Yashantika is an

Ajabuhi kingdom, so all Tapasi highborns in Vanpore should be killed. He put King Revant and Viraj to the task."

"Call them all back immediately," Tasvak thundered. "And inform me when Viraj and Revant are here."

In a few hours, the guard informed Tasvak that Viraj and Revant were back.

By now, Tasvak was livid. He stormed into the tent where Revant and Viraj were sitting. He wanted to confront them, but was shocked with what he saw.

Dishadevi was standing with a defiant look on her face. Revant, Viraj and Khoram were seated around her. They all went silent as Tasvak entered.

"What are you doing here, Queen Dishadevi?" asked Tasvak.

"We are persuading her to go with King Revant," said Viraj. "King Revant is smitten with her."

"We saved her from the pyre," added Revant. "The Tapasi priests were trying to immolate her with Jaskar Dharman's body. We killed the priests, and sent Jaskar Dharman's body to Kalsajja."

"You wicked man," said Dishadevi, with disgust.

She then turned towards Tasvak.

"Was this the promise you made to my husband?" she asked. "He asked you to kill him and spare his people. He asked you to allow his cremation."

"Hold your tongue!" shouted Khoram, standing up in Tasvak's support.

Tasvak looked at Khoram with such a rage that he let

out a soft whimper and receded into a corner.

"Forgive me, Queen Dishadevi," said Tasvak. "I apologize to you, and to the people of Vanpore. I was not aware of any of this."

"How did you let this happen?" Tasvak asked Viraj.

"Guru Trivit himself approved the raids," Viraj replied.

"Guru Trivit is not your king," thundered Tasvak.

"We did what was necessary," said Revant. "These people opposed the Ajabuhi faith. They raided the tribals and mistreated Dhatakis. We were just returning the favor."

"Disrupting the cremation, humiliating the queen, killing priests, destroying temples, burning people?" Tasvak asked in exasperation. "I always believed that war creates war heroes. But today I realized that war can create war villains, too."

Tasvak was trying hard to control himself, but could not hide his contempt towards Revant. Jaskar Dharman's words were ringing in his ears.

"King Revant, I am grateful for your help," he said curtly. "But it is no longer needed. I want you to leave Vanpore at this moment."

Revant had not expected this insult. Red in the face, he nodded at Tasvak, slowly got up, and left.

Tasvak then told Viraj and Khoram to apologize to Queen Dishadevi, and instructed his guards to respectfully escort her back to Vanpore.

As Tasvak walked out, he felt ashamed. But he had nobody to blame but himself. He wished he had listened to Zirosthi, and not trusted Trivit so much.

For years, Trivit had used Tasvak to spread Ajabuhi, and used the spread of Ajabuhi to increase his own power. Tasvak had been fine with this, because he knew that Trivit was using that power for the betterment of the people.

But that was only one face of Trivit. What he had seen today was the other face – the one wielding power without responsibility, who could do anything for his dominance over Jivavarta.

Tasvak now had a reason to believe Jaskar Dharman's words. Could Trivit have killed Avani? Could he have planned to get him killed to get control over Trishala? Everything seemed possible now.

The only way to be sure was to confront Trivit.

Tasvak spent the next few days closing the matters at Yashantika. He brought Yashantika under the control of Trishala, appointing Jivak as the king of Yashantika, and Dishadevi as the queen regent. To avoid rebellion of the Dhatakis, Tasvak suggested marriage between Khoram's daughter and King Jivak, who was reluctant but agreed as he had no choice.

Having thus resettled Yashantika, Tasvak sent his troops back to Trishala with Soumil, while he and Viraj, along with his Lokharo bodyguards, marched towards Vakshi.

79

THE GREATER GOOD

Tasvak stormed into the Ajabuhi monastery with his body-guards, leaving Viraj outside to keep watch. The evening prayers were about to start, and a large group of Ajabuhi followers had assembled seeking blessings from Guru Trivit.

Trivit warmly welcomed Tasvak, and asked him to join for the prayers.

Tasvak followed Trivit into the prayer hall. As he took a seat at the dais, he was surprised to see Revant seated beside Trivit. Revant noticed Tasvak, and fumed. He was still smarting from his insult at Vanpore.

Tasvak waited till the prayers were over, then stood up and addressed the people.

"I am pleased to announce that Rongcha, Yashantika, and Trishala are now united under me. I suppose I should be grateful to Guru Trivit, but one thing is stopping me from expressing my gratitude."

He glanced around at the people. They were looking at him curiously.

"Just before he died, King Jaskar Dharman made a confession. He told me that Guru Trivit was behind the death of Queen Avani."

The accusation caught the people by surprise. Outraged at the accusation on their guru, some of them stood up in protest. Tasvak raised his hands to silence them.

"I didn't believe it. I don't want to believe it. But then, why would a dying man lie? As Ajabuhi says, you should always confront your doubts."

Tasvak paused for a moment, and looked at Trivit.

"So here I am, asking Guru Trivit, whether he played any part in the murder of my beloved queen."

"This is ridiculous," somebody shouted. "How dare you to accuse our guru? He is like god to us."

"There are no gods in Ajabuhi," said Tasvak. "I am asking again. Guru Trivit, did you plan my beloved Avani's murder?"

"I request the guru to speak, and lay the king's doubts to rest," said a familiar voice. The voice belonged to Rudhata, Guru Sarvadni's former pupil. Rudhata was now an Ajabuhi monk.

"Have you lost your mind?" shouted Revant. "We are not allowed weapons in Vakshi, or I would have shown you the consequence of insulting Guru Trivit."

"Luckily, I don't follow such rules," said Tasvak, as his

fearsome Lokharo bodyguards flashed their weapons.

There was silence.

"How dare you break thousands of years of tradition?" somebody dared to ask.

"Ajabuhi is all about breaking traditions," replied Tasvak. "Now, Guru Trivit. What is the truth?"

All eyes on him, Trivit pondered for a moment, then nodded.

"Yes, I planned her death," said Trivit. "It was a sacrifice for the betterment of the people of Jivavarta, for the spread of Ajabuhi."

The followers started murmuring uneasily on hearing this. Tasvak was beside himself with rage.

"Why?" asked Tasvak. "What did she do to you? She was your follower, a kind person who never harmed anybody."

Trivit sighed, and looked at Tasvak.

"I had nothing against her," said Trivit. "But it was necessary. You were losing your ambition, and were becoming content with ruling Trishala. You even made an agreement with Jaskar Dharman to disallow Ajabuhi in Yashantika."

He then looked at his followers, and continued.

"Today, Ajabuhi has spread to Rongcha and Yashantika, ending the suffering of the people there. There are no human sacrifices in Rongcha anymore. There is no slavery, no mistreatment of Dhatakis in Yashantika anymore."

"For that you killed an innocent?" asked Tasvak, looking at Trivit in disbelief.

"Her death led to the upliftment of thousands of people," said Trivit. "We all are thankful for her sacrifice."

"You are a monster," raged Tasvak. "You are not fit to be a monk."

"I am the founder of Ajabuhi," said Trivit. "I decide who is fit to be an Ajabuhi monk."

"No, you are not the founder of Ajabuhi," said Tasvak. "You are just the one who gave it a name."

Tasvak could no longer hide his disgust.

"Way before you, there was one true Ajabuhi follower – Guru Sarvadni. Surely, there were thousands before him as well. They understood compassion, and cared for people's happiness. Guru Sarvadni helped people because he loved them, you help people so that they will love you. Guru Sarvadni used his faith to spread compassion, you use your faith to further your ambition."

"And you are the monster who killed Sarvadni," said Trivit.

Tasvak's face showed visible pain. This was one thing that he could never forgive himself for.

"Sarvadni gave his life for the greater good," said Tasvak. "You took another's life, an innocent life, for your own good."

"You are today the king of Trishala, Rongcha, and Yashantika with my support," said Trivit. "And this is how you repay me?"

"You supported me because it gave you power," said Tasvak. "You thought I will be a puppet in your hands. But when I refused to listen, you resented me, and my innocent wife had to pay the price."

Tasvak took a deep sigh.

"I have to stop you," he said. "I have to stop your lust for uncontrolled, irresponsible power."

Trivit shook his head.

"It was you who destroyed Rongcha, not me. It was you who killed the king of Yashantika, not me. People will never forgive you. Whenever the story of Jivavarta is written, you will always be a villain."

"Maybe I am a villain in your story, but I am a hero in mine," thundered Tasvak.

"Do you think that it is easy to stop Guru Trivit?" said Revant. "We will burn every person in Jivavarta who refuses to follow him."

"Will you really do that?" asked Tasvak.

"If it comes to that, we will!" replied Revant, with a tone of defiance.

A number of followers stood up and rallied behind Revant.

"Yes, we will!" shouted the supporters. "We will burn Jivavarta."

Tasvak was silent for a moment. He then stepped ahead, picked up a torch, and moved towards Trivit.

"What are you doing?" asked Revant. The defiance had evaporated.

"Burning Trivit," said Tasvak.

He looked at his bodyguards, and asked them to come forward.

"Kill whoever tries to save him," he ordered.

Revant looked at Tasvak in disbelief.

"King Tasvak has gone mad," he whimpered.

"You can't do this," somebody pleaded. "He is Guru Trivit!"

Trivit looked at the stunned supporters, then turned to Tasvak and smiled.

"You can kill me," said Trivit. "But you will never be able to kill my thoughts."

"I have no problem with your thoughts," said Tasvak. "It is your actions that I despise. I wish your actions were as respectable as your thoughts."

"My king, don't do this," said Viraj. Somebody had informed him of what was happening, and he had rushed in to stop Tasvak.

"Why not?" snapped Tasvak.

"Because it's not morally right," replied Viraj.

"If I don't kill Trivit now, he and his followers will burn every person who doesn't follow him," said Tasvak. "You saw what Revant did in Vanpore."

"But I know you, my king," pleaded Viraj. "You are better than this. I know your conscience will not allow you to commit such an act."

"My conscience is not worth more than the thousands of innocent lives they plan to take," said Tasvak. "I will stoop to any level to save those lives."

As the Lokharos cordoned around Trivit, the supporters started wailing.

They looked at their guru, who seemed to have accepted the fate, and stood unfazed watching Tasvak approach him.

"There is no point in crying," he said. "The king has made up his mind."

Trivit sat down, smiled, and closed his eyes. A calm descended over him as he started meditating.

Revant rushed towards Tasvak, and tried to snatch the torch. One of the bodyguards caught him and, with a wave of his weapon, slashed his throat. Revant dropped to the floor, and passed out.

Viraj watched tearfully as Tasvak moved towards Trivit, and set him on fire. Trivit sat calm and composed, deep in meditation, as the flames engulfed his body.

Tasvak stared at Trivit for a moment, took a deep breath, and slowly walked away. The deafening screams of the people around him, their cries of mercy, had no effect on him anymore.

80

THE GHOSTS OF THE PAST

The news of the killing of Guru Trivit and King Revant spread throughout Jivavarta. People were now afraid of King Tasvak, but also respected him for bringing peace to the land.

Tasvak appointed Rudhata as the chief monk of Ajabuhi. Having known Rudhata for long, Tasvak knew that he would bring Sarvadni's teachings and compassion into the fold of Ajabuhi.

The people of Adrika were initially outraged at the killing of Trivit and Revant, but the outrage died soon as they learned about the reason for the killings. Prince Briham, who had eyed the throne for decades, willingly accepted Trishala's dominance over Adrika in return for Tasvak appointing him the king.

Jivavarta had been united under one king for the first

time in its history, with Trishala as the capital. Queen Guduchi of Rongcha, King Jivak of Yashantika, King Briham of Adrika, and the chiefs of all the tribal settlements in Jivavarta now owed their allegiance to the king of Trishala. With a strong and benevolent ruler at the helm, Jivavarta was prospering – but some ghosts of the past remained.

Tasvak still yearned for Avani. He built a small shrine for her near the temple at the Nilabha lake, and visited it whenever he had a chance.

On one such day, as Tasvak was riding towards the shrine with his bodyguards, he was joined by Viraj and Soumil. Viraj seemed to be in mood for some fun.

"How about a race to the lake?" Viraj asked Tasvak.

Tasvak agreed, and his bodyguards took their positions behind him.

Viraj laughed.

"Why are your bodyguards accompanying you to the shrine?" he asked. "It's not that far away from the palace, and I don't think anyone will attack you in your own capital."

Tasvak gave it a thought, and nodded. He asked the bodyguards to wait for him at the palace. He then looked at Viraj, smiled, and kicked his horse. Viraj did the same, and Soumil followed. The horses galloped ahead with great speed.

Viraj reached the steps of the Nilabha lake first, with Tasvak close behind. Soumil was still far away.

"You were always a better rider than me," said Tasvak,

accepting his defeat cheerfully.

He jumped down from his horse, and started climbing the steps towards the shrine. Suddenly, he felt a sharp pain in his back. He fell forwards, and as he turned around, he saw Viraj with a sword in his hand.

Tasvak realized that his best friend had stabbed him.

Viraj moved beside Tasvak and prepared for the final stroke. Unable to move, and too severely injured to defend himself, Tasvak knew that he was going to die.

"Why?" he asked Viraj. "I was ready to die for you, but never realized that it was you who will kill me."

Viraj didn't answer, and raised his sword. But before Viraj could hit, his face went pale, and the sword dropped from his hand. He gave out a loud scream as he fell down beside Tasvak.

Reaching the steps after them, Soumil had seen Viraj in the act. Realizing what was happening, he had rushed forward and stabbed Viraj.

"Do you want me to kill him, my king?" asked Soumil, looking at Tasvak.

"You fool," screamed Viraj. "I am you uncle, your blood. Why are you doing this?"

"I am doing what I am supposed to do," answered Soumil.

"Should I kill him, my king?" Soumil asked again.

Tasvak nodded.

"Wait!" said Viraj. "Soumil, listen. Kill him, not me. We can be the rulers of Jivavarta. He would have done the same for power."

As Soumil raised his sword, he could see the fear in Viraj's eyes.

"You don't know him," Viraj was saying. "You don't know what all he has done to get this power. He killed Guru Sarvadni when it suited him, and he killed his step-brothers. And you remember how he killed Guru Trivit? He burned him alive."

Soumil did not respond. Viraj was getting desperate.

"Think, Soumil," Viraj mumbled, as fast as he could. "Think. You will be the crown prince. We will rule. Kill him."

Soumil shook his head.

"Remember, I saved your life once," Viraj pleaded. "Have mercy on your uncle Daras. Mercy, my nephew."

Soumil was not listening. He thrust the sword into Viraj's neck.

Soumil then tried to attend to Tasvak's wound. The wound was deep, but he succeeded in stopping the oozing blood. Feeling a little better, Tasvak leaned against the wall.

"You will be fine soon, my king," said Soumil, tears rolling down his face. "I know that you are invincible."

Tasvak gave a muted sigh.

"I am not going to survive," he said. "Tasvak was invincible against his greatest enemies, but was killed by his best friend."

"No, my king," said Soumil. "I cannot let you die like this."

"Take me to Avani's shrine," Tasvak said.

"Let me take you to the court physician," Soumil urged.

"No," said Tasvak. "Take me to Avani's shrine. I want to die with her beside me."

With great difficulty, Soumil carried Tasvak to Avani's shrine on the hill beside the lake. Tasvak sat in front of Avani's statue.

"Soumil," Tasvak asked, "do you know who is the hero of a story?"

"The one who is brave and honorable," replied Soumil.

Tasvak laughed silently. He recalled his time in Vakshi, long back, when someone had asked him that question, and he had given a similar answer.

"No," said Tasvak. "The hero of a story is the one who survives to tell the story."

He looked at Soumil, and patted his head lovingly.

"And that's going to be you. You are going to succeed me. You are going to be the king of Jivavarta, and you are going to complete my work. My grandfather Zirosthi and monk Rudhata will help you."

Soumil looked at Tasvak with tears in his eyes.

"Promise me," said Tasvak, with great effort. "Promise me that you will take care of my son Abhik, and teach him my values."

"I promise, my king," said Soumil.

Tasvak smiled.

"I will rest now," he said.

Tasvak looked longingly at Avani's statue one last time, closed his eyes, and breathed his last.

81

EPILOGUE

Soumil succeeded Tasvak to the throne of Trishala. He had a long and eventful reign, but that is a whole different story.

Today, when travelers to Trishala visit the Nilabha lake, they find a statue of the great king with the following inscription:

> Tasvak, the husband of loving wife Avani, the king of Trishala, the conqueror of Rongcha and Yashantika, the unifier of Jivavarta, and the protector of the oppressed, who was loved by his people and died for them.
>
> *Built by the order of . . .*
> *Soumil, the Emperor of Jivavarta*

TIMINGILA: A STRANGE FISH

This is the story of an ancient sea,
And the monster, who made everyone flee.
Timingila was a strange fish,
Being free was his only wish.

Along came the killer shark,
Whose nature was too dark.
The shark tried to eat him,
But it was Timingila, who did eliminate him.

Along came the wily octopus,
Whose arms moved with a terrifying rush.
The octopus tried to mutilate him,
But it was Timingila, who did eliminate him.

Along came the devious whale,
Who knew that he will never fail.

The whale tried to bait him,
But it was Timingila, who did eliminate him.

Thus, to remain free,
Timingila went on a killing spree.
Cause Timingila was a strange fish,
Being free was his only wish.

THE TRISHALA WARRIORS

No brooding over old worries,
Let's start a new series.
Forget about all negativities,
Think of new possibilities.
Here to conquering new frontiers,
We are the Trishala warriors!

Adapted as a New Year Greeting

No brooding over old worries,
Let's start a new series.
Forget about all negativities,
Think of new possibilities.
Here to conquering a new frontier,
That's all I wish in the upcoming new year!

Acknowledgments / Credits

I thank Heema Sheth for her help with the character names.

The cover includes the image "Harshavardhana Circa AD 606-647" by Classical Numismatic Group, Inc., licensed under Creative Commons Attribution-Share Alike 3.0 (CC-BY-SA-3.0) via Wikimedia Commons.

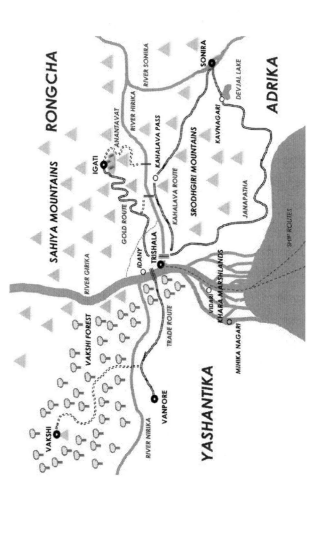

MAP OF JIVAVARTA

Made in the USA
Columbia, SC
16 August 2023

21717799R00178